A True History
of the Captivation,
Transport to Strange Lands,
& Deliverance of
Hannah Guttentag

Also by Josh Russell

Yellow Jack
My Bright Midnight

A TRUE HISTORY

of the
Captivation,
Transport
to
Strange Lands,
& Deliverance
of
Hannah Guttentag

JOSH RUSSELL

DZANC
BOOKS

Dzanc Books
1334 Woodbourne Street
Westland, MI 48186
www.dzancbooks.org

This is a work of fiction. While the author intends the geographies of
Tennessee, New York, Louisiana, Ohio, and Nebraska to be realistic,
the characters in this book are fictional. Any resemblance between these
characters and anyone living or dead is coincidental.

ISBN-13: 978-1-936873-72-2
Cover design by Amanda Jane Jones and Steven Seighman.
Design and composition by Snack Bar.
Printed in the United States of America by Edwards Brothers, Inc.

Library of Congress Cataloging-in-Publication Data
Russell, Josh.
  A true history of the captivation, transport to strange lands, &
  deliverance of Hannah Guttentag / Josh Russell.
    p. cm.
  ISBN 978-1-936873-72-2
  I. Title.
  PS3568.U76677T78 2012
  813'.54—dc23
  2012019720

9 8 7 6 5 4 3 2 FIRST PRINTING

ACKNOWLEDGMENTS
Long overdue—since 1988 or thereabouts—are heartfelt thanks to
Howard Norman for making me read Junichiro Tanizaki's *The Key,* and
Maurice Bennett (may he rest in peace) for introducing me to Mary
Rowlandson's narrative of her captivity. More timely but no less genuine
is my gratitude for the support of everyone at Dzanc Books, especially
Steven Gillis, Dan Wickett, and Matt Bell, and for the invaluable boost
provided by a Georgia State University Professional Leave.

Publication of this book is made possible in part by grants from the
National Endowment for the Arts and the Michigan Council for
the Arts and Cultural Affairs.

For Kathryn

On the afternoon of February 18, 1990, six weeks into my last
semester at the University of Tennessee, I received a letter
offering me admission to the graduate program at Cornell.
I was stunned, then ecstatic. I'd been told to be proud of my
4.0, my Phi Beta Kappa key, and my ninety-seventh-percen-
tile GRE scores, but to apply to UGA and Kentucky and be
happy if I got in anywhere. For the most part I did as advised.
Filling out Cornell's forms was the extent of my application
rebellion. When I hurried to the English department and
shared the good news with my UT professors, they looked
shocked, or offered halfhearted congratulations, or refused
to believe it could be true.

One pipe-smoking graybeard, whose tedious lectures on
Melville and Dickinson included dozens of slides of their
historic homes, asked if I'd checked the postmark to make
sure the letter came from Ithaca, then suggested, "Maybe it's
one of your buddies pulling a prank."

"Maybe you're an asshole," I said, and the easy way the
obscenity rolled off my tongue seemed confirmation I was
better suited to the Ivy League than the land-grant back-
waters I'd been told by this caricature and his cronies I'd be
lucky if allowed to attend—their alma maters, in more than
several cases.

When I called my mother in Nashville, she worried it
wasn't a good idea for me to go so far from home, suggested
I wait to hear from Auburn and FSU. "Fuck Auburn, Mom,"
I told her, practicing my new badass Back East persona. "And
fuck FSU, too."

The next morning I called the Ithaca *Journal* and doubled
my drawl to charm a guy into reading me the want ads. Three

women were looking for summer live-in nannies. The first asked where I was calling from, and when I said Knoxville, she told me she loved Faulkner and Eudora Welty. I didn't inform her they were from Mississippi. She hired me.

February came to its end, March passed, then April, and as May faded, I donned a mortarboard and posed with my mother for snapshots.

My charge was a five-year-old boy named Kree Carey. The Careys lived in a house next to the one behind which Nabokov tried to burn the manuscript of *Lolita* but was stopped by his wife. "No historical marker to back me up," Mark Carey lamented, "but I swear it's true." Mark and his wife, Helena, were librarians at Ithaca College, their house was full of books, they grew their own tomatoes and peas and eggplants in the front yard, cooked vegetarian meals, churned their own ice cream, and I loved them and took them for granted. Meatless breakfasts, homemade ricotta, no TV—this was what I expected from New York. The weather, too, was so foreign that it made sense: June evenings so cool I needed to buy a sweater at the Salvation Army store, June noontimes sunny and lovely as spring in Tennessee. One morning my mother complained via long distance it was ninety degrees in Nashville. That afternoon it rained in Ithaca and got cold enough to start the radiators knocking.

Kree was silly and rambunctious and liked to take his clothes off. At six every morning he moseyed into my tiny room wearing nothing but a cowboy hat and red boots, ready to face the day. I tried to take him to the city pool, but he couldn't be convinced to keep his trunks on. If I turned away to pay for pizza, he was bare-chested when I turned back. In the end I gave up and took him to the Cascadilla Gorge where little kids skinny-dipped in the creek that ran through the middle of town.

One afternoon in early July I was sitting at the edge the creek, reading *Lolita* through sunglasses and hoping Kree and his friend Oscar weren't masturbating under cover of the water.

A male voice asked, "Is Cornell up *there?*" I'd been in Ithaca for almost six weeks, but I was still amazed by the beauty of the gorge's waterfalls and cliffs and the steps cut into the rock, beauty that was clearly amazing this guy with the strong jaw and the big eyebrows.

"It sure is." I was pleased he'd mistaken me for a local.

He looked away from the falls, at me, and then over my shoulder. "Your kids are beating off," he said, before starting up toward campus.

The next day Kree was with Oscar and his nanny, and I spent my afternoon off poking around the English department. The deserted halls of Goldwin Smith were cool and quiet and dimly lit. I read *New Yorker* cartoons on professors' doors, peeked into empty classrooms, and tried to imagine what was soon to come. I ran into the guy from the gorge apparently doing the same.

"Hey. You found it."

He looked confused. "Found what?"

"Cornell. Yesterday you asked me if it was up here. Remember? Then you told me Kree and Oscar were beating off."

His face reddened and I smiled and stuck out my hand. "Hannah Guttentag."

He smiled back and shook. "Frank Doyle."

I liked the gap between his front teeth.

I showed him the Green Dragon, the coffee shop in the basement of Sibley Hall, ate late lunch with him at the Indian place right off campus where the Careys went on Wednesday nights, agreed to meet downtown for a beer and drew him a map on the back of a takeout menu.

I picked up Kree from Oscar's house—his parents were two women, lawyers—and from one of Oscar's moms received a report of the boys' "self-pleasuring." I'd read Helena's books on child development and agreed with their authors it was a bad idea to tell Kree it was wrong to do what he and Oscar did, but I felt I needed to find a way to explain decorum and societal expectations to a five-year-old. Helena and Mark laughed when I told them all of this.

"Keep your pants on and your hands outside of them, at least in public," Mark told his son.

"Okay," Kree agreed, kicking off his shoes and struggling out of his shirt.

Masturbation was on my mind when I met Frank at the bar after dinner. Four beers later—and after much talk on various theories of sexuality, the role of autoeroticism in the development of young men and women, and the remarkable lack of self-love in serious literature—Frank paid the tab, and I led him to DeWitt Park, found a bench away from pedestrian traffic and streetlights, eased down his zipper, and pushed up my skirt. It was thrilling, like a return to junior year of high school and my first serious boyfriend, to a time of simple, electric sex, Wes Owen touching me in the backseat of his Ford Escort while I touched him. With the tips of two fingers, Frank gently rubbed my clitoris, the whereabouts of which had escaped Wes.

It was nice to be in the dark, sitting side by side, crickets chirping and lightning bugs rising and blinking, Frank's free arm around my shoulders, his Levi's rough against my bare right knee, my fingers atop his so we almost held hands as he brought me closer and closer and closer. Frank came first, pulsing in my fist and gasping through his teeth, and I quickly followed.

I left him in the park and walked home whistling, proud of myself for being too cool to demand a number, force a number upon him, suggest brunch. This was the new Hannah, Ivy League Hannah, Hannah who didn't blink when told Oscar had two moms, Hannah who thoughtfully weighed the pros and cons of Kree's public nudity, Hannah who listened to Helena and Mark groaning in their marital bed and idly wondered who was on top. New York Hannah, Cornell Hannah, Hannah whose Southern drawl was mysterious—no cowgirl hick from Tennessee. Hannah whistling "Every Day I Write the Book," whistling "Please, Please, Please, Let Me Get What I Want."

3

On the last Saturday in July I went out to dinner with Marci, Oscar's nanny. I thought it was a preemptive going-away celebration. Kree's school-year nanny, Bess, was coming back in a week, and for several days I'd felt like my time in the Carey house was already over and I was looking back at it. I missed Kree while standing beside him as we waited for the stoplight to change, missed Helena and Mark while they sat across from me in the breakfast nook reading the Sunday *Times*. They weren't going anywhere, and the apartment I'd put a deposit on was only a five-minute walk from their house, but I couldn't stop feeling premature nostalgia when watching Helena picking tomatoes, or Mark at the curb, sorting the mail, or Kree, in only yellow rain boots and a Red Sox cap, a Lincoln Log in his fist, chasing the neighbor's cat across the lawn.

"I miss them already," I admitted to Marci, as the waiter walked away after taking our orders.

"Miss who?" Marci asked, then quickly confided that she and one of Oscar's moms were having an affair, and she worried she'd be fired if the other mom found out.

I was dumbfounded. I'd listened to Mark and Helena's bedsprings, but I'd never considered I could help make the springs sing. I wasn't completely sure which of Oscar's moms was Claire and which was Debbie, and so I wasn't sure with whom Marci was sleeping. I imagined all three in bed together—which I knew was homophobic as well as factually inaccurate—and that caused me to imagine being in bed with both Helena and Mark.

I focused on the least sexual part of Marci's confession. "You're worried you'll get fired?"

"Debbie's wicked jealous."

"You think Claire will confess?" I felt a rush of relief when I remembered Claire's green eyes, Debbie's brown.

"No way. She knows Deb'll kick her out, take her for every penny she's got, get sole custody."

"Poor Oscar." When I saw the look on Marci's face, I knew that wasn't the response she'd hoped for.

"You were the wrong person to come to for advice," she said, then got up and stomped off.

The waiter set my appetizer in front of me, put down a plate of fried calamari before Marci's empty chair. I ate a bite of goat cheese tart and tried not to look at the tweedy couple sitting at the next table. Through the restaurant's window I watched Frank walk past. I hadn't seen him in weeks, not since the night in the park. The waiter was nowhere to be seen, so I got up and nodded to the tweeds, and they smiled back kindly as if they assumed Marci and I had just had a lovers' spat. I walked out, emboldened by their smiles. This was Ithaca. Nannies slept with their female employers, patrons in fancy restaurants felt bad for young women when their girlfriends left in a huff, Hannah Guttentag didn't pay for her appetizer.

"Hey!" I yelled at Frank's back. "Hey, *asshole.*"

Every man in the street turned to me.

He'd been living in a pup tent in the Buttermilk Falls campground. His beater Datsun had run out of gas when he pulled into the parking lot a month before, and he'd been waiting on a check. To make the trip from the state park into town he had to break camp, lock his gear in the trunk, and walk. His eyebrows were wilder than I remembered. They looked like Beckett's.

"You bought me four beers."

Frank smiled. "Bankrupted me."

"You!" someone shouted. I looked over my shoulder. The waiter was hustling down the sidewalk, waving the check like a little flag.

"Run," I told Frank, stepping out of my shoes. I picked them up and grabbed his hand and we hurried into the night.

"Uncool!" hollered the waiter. "*Uncool!*"

We slowed a few blocks later when it was clear the waiter had given up the chase.

"I was reading *Pride and Prejudice* at a picnic table," Frank said, "and these two guys stopped and asked me if I was trying to get picked up, or if I was a grad student."

"Those are the only two reasons a man reads Jane Austen in public?"

"I guess so." We crossed a bridge under which a creek burbled. "They're grad students—or they were. Stanley just got a job in Kansas, and he and Charles were making one last visit to Buttermilk to swim." We were still holding hands. Frank nodded toward a little bungalow with a porch swing. "They paid the rent through August." He rattled his pocket change and found the key.

The rooms were empty and our footsteps echoed. I followed him into the kitchen and he opened the fridge. It was filled with food and beer. He handed me a tallboy. "Check came," he explained.

We went out on the porch and sat in the swing. I told him about Marci and he shook his head. "This place"—he gestured widely toward the dark street—"is on another planet."

"I'm scared I'm not smart enough to be here," I admitted.

"Oh thank God," he said. "Me too."

We took turns fetching beers from the fridge, took turns telling our stories. He was from Cleveland. His father sold real estate, his mother was a housewife, his little brother played guard on his high school basketball team, and they all died in a car crash when Frank was a sophomore at Ohio State.

We swung in silence for a few long minutes, both of us looking out into the dark while the chains of the porch swing creaked, then he told me he ended up graduating from Cleveland State and then got a M.A. there. He'd paid his way working as a carpenter and a roofer. He was sure everyone else at Cornell was going to have graduated from Yale and judge him a rube.

"Stanley went to Haverford," Frank said. "I don't even know where that is."

"Philadelphia, I think." I added M.A. to B.A., figured with the transfer it might've taken him five years to finish his bachelor's, maybe six, then two for the master's, and guessed he was twenty-six or seven—four or five years older than me.

"How about Bowdoin? Charles went to Bowdoin."

"Maine, maybe? I think Haverford might've been founded by Quakers."

I got two more beers and told him about being insulted by my UT professors, told him about growing up in Nashville, made sure to mention I was in debt for in-state tuition, that until the day he died of a heart attack when I was a college junior, my father taught junior high social studies at a school named for a Ford dealer, that my mother was still a secretary for a State Farm agent in Antioch. I told him about the Careys and about Kree's public nudity and he laughed.

We talked about movies, Saturday morning cartoons we'd loved as kids, which sugary breakfast cereals had been our favorites. When I said, "I'm starving," Frank fetched me a family-sized box of Honeycomb and I ate it like popcorn.

We were laughing about Hong Kong Phooey, singing the absurd Orientalist theme song—*Hong Kong Phooey, number one super guy! Hong Kong Phooey, quicker than the human eye!*—when a man in pajamas walked up the porch stairs and said, "It's two o'clock in the fucking morning."

Through the haze of a six-pack he looked like the waiter. "I am so sorry," I told him. "How much do I owe you?"

He stared at me, then said, "Just shut up and we'll call it even," and walked back into the darkness.

"Oh, *neighbor*," I realized out loud.

Frank took my hand and silently led me to the bedroom where he unrolled a sleeping bag on the floor. I lay down beside him and tried to remember if the condom I'd put in my purse after the night in the park was still there, or if I'd taken it out—I'd worried Kree would find it during his daily investigations—tried to remember where my purse even was, hoped I hadn't left it at the restaurant, hoped I'd shaved my legs, then hoped I hadn't, so it didn't seem I was planning to run into him and end up in a situation where he would be touching my legs, tried to think of some way to let him know I wanted to do it without appearing loose or aggressive. I touched his hand and said softly, "I like you."

He snored.

I woke in a sun-blasted room to a bumping and squeaking reminiscent of Mark and Helena's bedsprings. I jerked fully awake and checked my watch: eight forty-five. Outside the uncurtained window a little girl wearing a tutu and T-shirt bounced on a trampoline in the backyard next door. I left Frank asleep on the floor and hurried to the Careys'. Kree and Mark were sitting on the porch steps.

"You look like shit," Mark told me. "I'm late for work."

"When's Bess coming back?" Kree asked his dad.

4

Weeks passed and we didn't again go past first base. Frank held my hand when we went for twilight walks, left funny notes on the pillow when we spent the night together and he had to get up before dawn to leave for work while I was asleep—he was roofing for a contractor in Cayuga Heights until the semester began. We kissed on his sleeping bag while Hill Street Blues reruns played on his tiny black and white TV; we kissed on my new futon; we kissed in his Datsun, parked by the lake in the moonlight. August wore on and we kissed and kissed and kissed and never got close to doing what we'd done in the park. It was refreshing. UT boys began with a hand up the skirt, down the pants. Frank kissed my chin, my eyelids, behind my ears.

The night he slipped his hand under my blouse, ran his fingertips up my spine (causing a chill to shake me), and popped the clasp on my bra, I was so shocked I pulled away and crossed my arms over my chest. I came to my senses when I saw his frightened face and I laughed—at myself, at him—then unbuttoned my shirt. Frank's wide eyes made me laugh again. Nevertheless, we kept our pants on.

5

The grad student mixer began before Frank would be home from the job site, so we agreed to meet there. The party was on a redwood deck behind the house of a professor I couldn't identify in the crowd. I wore a cheery sundress and matching yellow hairband while almost every other woman was dressed in black. I clutched a six-pack of High Life and wished someone would talk to me.

A chubby guy in a tie-dyed Bob Marley T-shirt looked me up and down, smirking, and then said, "That's an awfully proletariat brew for a little lady in such a bourgeois frock."

A woman with an asymmetrical haircut snorted and sipped white wine.

"I'm Hannah," I told her, hoping she'd save me from the jerk stroking his goatee and staring at my boobs.

"Charmed," she said, and turned away.

"My name's Todd," the guy in the Bob shirt volunteered. His eyes were bloodshot, his breath terrible. "I do medieval, but writing poetry's really my fort."

"Isn't it pronounced *for-tay?*" I asked.

The woman snorted again, and I wished Frank would show up, wished I hadn't worn the yellow dress, wished the woman would stop snorting.

I walked to the washtub of ice on the other side of the deck. When I looked down at bottles of chardonnay and German and Mexican beer, I felt like a hayseed for bringing cans of Miller. I hid the High Life behind a pot of basil and opened a Beck's. No one would make eye contact with me.

I tried not to stare at a man and a woman who were kissing with the kind of clumsy public passion I'd seen only at frat parties and Mardi Gras. What really made me look was the towheaded baby strapped to the man's chest. The woman had to bend over the child's head to french the guy. Todd tapped me on the shoulder and I was so embarrassed he'd caught me staring that all I did when he held out one of my sweating tallboys and said, "Makes your pussy drippy, doesn't it?" was accept the beer and take a long swallow.

"What did you just say to her?"

The low hum of conversation stopped and the kissing couple pulled away from each other. Frank's hair was combed straight back and still wet. He wore a Black Flag T-shirt and cut-offs and flip-flops and mirrored sunglasses and looked like he'd just showered after working construction.

The snorting woman came and stood close beside me.

"Her?" Todd asked everyone but Frank. "You mean, what did I say to her?"

Frank took off his sunglasses and put them in his back pocket. "You need to apologize."

"Listen, dude," Todd said, "I don't want to have to kick your ass because some twat in a sundress got her feelings hurt."

"Not much of an apology," the snorting woman judged.

Todd snapped, "Shut up, Joanie." Someone muttered *fucking moron,* and he bounced on the balls of his feet like he'd been cheered, not jeered.

"You're a dick, Todd," the man with the infant on his chest said.

"Kick him in the nuts," Joanie suggested, but it was not clear to whom.

Todd threw a clumsy punch and Frank caught his wrist and twisted his arm behind him and pushed him down to the deck, then pinned him with a knee across his shoulders. I squeezed my can of Miller and fought back the urge to groan joyously.

Todd wailed, "I'm being assaulted!"

"Everyone hates you, Todd," the guy with the baby announced. There was a murmur of agreement. "Many of us have fantasized about doing much worse than this to you."

"That's Professor Whitfield," Joanie whispered into my ear.

"Are you seriously going to twist my arm until I say uncle?" Todd asked, trying—and failing—to sound cool.

Frank cranked his arm and Todd brayed, "*Sorry.*"

"Apology accepted?" Frank asked me nonchalantly.

"Accepted," I agreed.

We stayed at the party long enough for me to finish a second High Life and for Frank to drink one too. Fredrick Whitfield, our host, passed the baby to Sabrina, his wife, and sipped Miller with us while Todd sulked alone in the yard with a bottle of Beaujolais. Professor Whitfield wanted us to call him Rick, wanted to know where we were from, wanted to believe Frank and I had never before met.

After Rick made us admire the antique MG roadster in his garage, I asked Frank, "Buy you dinner for defending my honor?"

The professor slapped Frank on the back and grinned like he was sending his son off to prom.

The Datsun was parked at the bottom of the steep driveway, and before he put the key in the ignition, Frank put his hand high on my thigh.

I pushed it higher. "I wasn't serious about dinner."

"Hoped so," he said.

In the kitchen half of my one-room apartment, he pulled the yellow dress up over my head, started when he found me braless, then jerked down my underwear, pressed me against the refrigerator with his knee between my legs, and kissed me more deeply than he had the many, many times he'd kissed me before.

When the kiss ended, I gasped, "Bed," and nearly fell when I tripped over the underpants around my ankles.

I kicked books and folded laundry to the floor while he ducked out of his shirt and dropped his shorts. He was lean and beautiful and I felt flabby until he looked at me—legs parted, waiting—and swallowed.

After so many nights of rubbing against each other never more than topless, finally having all of his skin against all of mine made me feel beyond naked. We rolled and kissed and fumbled and he nearly ended up inside me. When I told him to fetch a condom from the medicine cabinet, he sprang from the futon and ran for the bathroom. I watched his narrow behind, his bouncing penis.

He came back with the box and stood beside the bed, a sheepish look on his face. "I've never done this before," he said.

I was shocked. "You've never worn a condom?" Warnings from campus health center posters and brochures filled my head and I covered myself like an Old Master's prim Eve, arm across my chest, hand hiding my crotch. Frank pretended to study the instructions, and, relieved, I understood what he'd never done.

"Never?"

"Disappointed?"

"Are you disappointed I have?"

He looked baffled by the question.

I reached up and took the box. "Lie down," I told him. It didn't take long for both of us to grow excited again. I unrolled the Trojan onto him, kissed his bellybutton, got on top, guided him inside, then put my hands on his shoulders and began to move.

Frank's eyes were open so wide it looked like he was making fun. He whispered, "Where do I put my hands?"

I wanted him to touch my breasts, but said, "Anywhere you want."

He put them on my hips, pushed deeper into me. When I grunted softly, he asked in a worried voice, "You okay?"

"That was a happy noise," I promised.

I thought about how I liked him, how I liked we'd waited, how I liked being his first, how I liked being in charge, how exciting it would be to have the choice to give up control—and how I didn't have to give up control. I could do whatever I wanted, I could say whatever I wanted. I could talk dirty, hiss words I'd hated hearing on the beery breath of UT boys—but I didn't want to talk dirty, and I didn't want to hear Frank talk dirty. His hands slid down over my hips until he was palming my butt.

"That okay?"

"I like that." Simply speaking calmly during the act was so novel it turned me on even more. "Now touch my breasts." When he did, I pondered what else to ask for.

I knew I was thinking too much, that I should stop thinking and just enjoy the best sex I'd ever had, but thinking about it was not diminishing the pleasure. In fact, being comfortable enough to think while having sex, rather than having to brace for the moment Frank would say *cunt* or suggest I *suck it*, increased my pleasure exponentially.

My orgasm was better than the one from the night in the park. The quick chirp I made would've embarrassed me had I been with anyone else, but I was with Frank.

His eyes were squeezed closed and his mouth was puckered in concentration. He moved his hands to the base of my spine where they rested heavily. A second orgasm was rippling deep in my belly, each ripple clearing my mind and making me feel like I was glowing. I stopped thinking.

I leaned down and pressed a nipple between his pursed lips and he opened his eyes in wonder and I felt him throbbing inside me and I ground my hips hard against his and the last ripple crested and broke over me and my hands slipped off his shoulders and I fell onto him so heavily I smashed the wind out of his lungs.

I felt his heart hammering against me. His shoulder smelled so good I licked it.

"Wow," he gasped. "Is it always that awesome?"

"Yes," I lied, wished it were true, hoped it might be true with him.

6

Someone was knocking. I opened my eyes to the sight of the back of Frank's head. I kissed said head, slid from bed half-asleep, pulled on a pair of pajama pants, and picked up the first T-shirt I stepped on. The apartment was a twenty-by-ten-foot rectangle divided into three rooms: ten-by-ten bedroom/living room, five-by-ten kitchen, five-by-ten bathroom. The bedroom floor was industrial gray carpet squares, the kitchen and bath tan linoleum squares. I crossed bedroom carpet and kitchen lino and opened the door to find smiling Todd holding a Dunkin' Donuts bag. I smelled chocolate icing and my mouth watered.

His eyes dropped and widened and I crossed my arms over my chest until I realized he was gawking at Frank's Black Flag shirt, not my breasts. I didn't hear him, but I knew from the flabbergasted look on Todd's face that Frank was behind me. When he stepped past to take the sack of doughnuts, I learned he'd come to the door naked.

"Dude," Frank said, "no coffee?"

7

In one of my first classes at Cornell, a professor named Presley implored us to take risks, *make it new*, explore the interstices between criticism, poetry, theory, philosophy—even between visual art and text. I left the seminar room exhilarated, excitement filling the interstice between sexual arousal and intellectual titillation. I rushed home to the apartment I'd shared with Frank since the night we finally slept together, pulled books from the shelves, found rubber cement and scissors and the needlepoint kit my mother had given me when I was twelve. I wrote some paragraphs in longhand with a fountain pen filled with green ink, typed others on my yard-sale Royal, cut lines of poetry from Xeroxed coursepacks I'd saved over the years. I freehanded copies of Blake illustrations, traced Bauhaus and Frank Lloyd Wright floor plans.

Frank came home from his class and I shoved him into bed.

After, naked, I went back to work, sex revving me up. He brought me a peanut butter sandwich; he made me put on a shirt and some sweatpants; he told me to come to bed. Blinking, I looked at the clock. It was three a.m. In my hands was a book the size and thickness of a deck of cards, spine sewn with butterscotch needlepoint thread, cover made from maroon leather I'd cut from a thrift-store purse.

"Make it new," I told him.

"Take off those pants," he countered.

The next morning I waited at Professor Presley's door, passed the book to him with shaking hands when he arrived forty-five minutes after his office hour was scheduled to begin. He opened it and touched his finger to the first page.

"An ellipsis is dot-space-dot-space-dot, not dot-dot-dot."

I was heartbroken and disgusted; I didn't ask him to give me my book back.

I wandered over to the Green Dragon and saw Joanie sitting in the corner with two other women who wore the same asymmetrical hairdo. All three were dressed in black from turtleneck to tights. They looked like backup singers. I hadn't encountered snorting Joanie since the party, and I turned to leave, too exhausted to suffer any more humiliation.

"Hannah!" she called brightly. "Come sit with us!" She was smiling. I wanted coffee. I nodded, bought a cup, and joined the group. Joanie introduced me to Sam and Nat.

"Having fun yet?" Nat asked.

I didn't know what to say. "I just—Presley?"

The three women rolled their eyes. "*Make it new,*" Sam mocked.

"Interrogate the interstices," Nat added.

Joanie shook her head. "When we had his class last year, he gave everyone A-minuses, except for his babysitter. She got an A."

I didn't mention my little book. "I took him seriously when he told us to take risks."

"Have you read his stuff?" Nat asked.

Sam and Joanie laughed.

I didn't get the joke. "What's so funny?"

"His 'scholarship' is about the pets of the Romantics," Sam explained. "He's published five books—*five*—about Byron and Shelley's dogs and cats."

"Somebody had a tortoise," Nat said. "Maybe Coleridge?

Each sip of coffee was like a minute of deep sleep. Buttery September sun slanted into the basement café. I listened to Joanie and Sam and Nat say smart, snide things about TV shows and books and movies and professors, and it became clear to me it would be at times like this, in coffee shops and bars and restaurants and at parties—and alone—that I would live the life of the mind I'd imagined living when I first got the letter from Cornell. When Presley ignored the beauty of my lovely little book to note the spacing of an ellipsis, I decided to quit, but hearing these women talk and laugh made me change my mind. I loved Ithaca, I might love Frank, and I was willing to suffer to keep what I loved. I would go to class that afternoon and on the many afternoons to come, I would read dull articles, listen to dull lectures, suffer insincere challenges to take risks and disingenuous calls to make it new offered by men who risked nothing and made new nothing.

8

Frank was a hyper-organized neat freak with a system for everything—dishwashing, trash-emptying, floor-scrubbing. He had a system for sorting dirty laundry, another for folding clean. One day I came home to find my clothes hung alphabetically from black to white, short sleeves before long, shirts before skirts before pants. When he made instant espresso, he wiped down the stovetop and the countertop and the knobs on the sink faucet while the cup cooled, drank his coffee standing on the porch, watching the birds at the feeder in the neighbor's backyard, and then scrubbed, rinsed, and toweled dry the mug, the spoon he'd used to measure and stir powdered coffee, and the kettle in which he'd boiled water.

At first I found his routines funny, like watching an overwound toy monkey frantically clapping its cymbals, and it was nice to know exactly where my blue shirt was, where to find my tartan skirt (primarily black, though it had enough green in its plaid to vex Frank). Then one day I made the mistake of washing dishes while he shaved. I was enjoying the warm water running over my hands while I lazily rinsed a fork and looked out the window over the sink. The birds Frank watched while sipping his morning coffee were harassing the squirrel gorging on their seed.

Frank tapped my shoulder. His cheeks were pink and smooth, but he still wore a precise Vandyke of lather. He had a shaving system, clearly. "If you have an alternate dishwashing system, that's fine, but if all you're going to do is waste water and soap and not really clean the plates, then respect my system and just leave the dirty dishes alone."

It was our first fight, and there wasn't much to it: "Fuck you," I said, then dropped the fork and walked out without closing the taps. I was barefoot and furious. "*An alternate dishwashing system?*" I said out loud. Once around the block and I was still pissed.

It would've been one thing if all of Frank's systems involved doing things diligently and correctly, but they didn't. He boasted about skimming assigned readings and making the first comment in class in order to appear over-prepared and overeager. Sitting in the Green Dragon, I watched him slosh coffee into his saucer and then use his cup to stamp rings on random pages of his students' essays before awarding each a B+ without comments, a dozen papers graded in five minutes. My meager fellowship didn't involve teaching, and out of pity for the freshman he was supposed to be instructing, I convinced Frank to let me do his grading. As I neared the end of my third circuit of the block, I wondered if I annoyed him. Was it hard to share 200 square feet with a slob? Did it get under his skin to spend all his time with a grind?

When I walked in, Frank was wiping the window over the sink with a Windex-dampened paper towel. "Listen," I told him, "I'll rinse my cereal bowl and my spoon, and I'll read Kant in translation, but we can never take a class together."

9

Frank exhausted my patience by the end of October. His systems were legion, and the glee with which he ignored his scholarship made me feel like a sucker for studying. When he blew off writing a paper for his Victorian poetry seminar to have uninterrupted time to construct an elaborate Halloween costume crow's-head mask out of chicken wire, papier-mâché, and feathers plucked from a black boa he bought at a garage sale, I decided to dump him. Then I missed a period. A drugstore test told me I wasn't pregnant, but the box admitted it might be too early to know for sure.

I didn't tell Frank or anyone else. We'd paired up so quickly neither of us had made any other friends, and I didn't feel like calling long distance to hear my mother cry or berate me. I went to the Halloween party at Professor Whitfield's where Frank's mask earned him first prize in the costume contest—a bottle of gin and a jar of cocktail onions—and where Todd—drunk, high, fat—suggested I blow him in the bushes. I was too tired to tattle. "Ask Joanie," I suggested. I found an empty Bud longneck without a cigarette butt in it, rinsed it, surreptitiously filled it with 7-Up, and sipped soda all night while Frank got wasted. I was sure I was pregnant. I'd never been more than two days late, and a week had passed since my October period was due. Frank toppled into the sunken living room and ruined his mask and I made up my mind to have an abortion over Christmas vacation and break up with him over the phone.

I invented a system of my own to get through the end of the semester. Part one of the system involved having as much sex as possible. This part worked well simply because Frank was unlikely to lecture me on a proper system of cleaning toilets while we were screwing. Part two of my system was cloistering myself in a library carrel where I read, wrote, and napped. *Bed and Books*—a secret society, membership one.

November passed quickly. We ate Thanksgiving dinner at Denny's—a tradition, Frank claimed. I guessed it had something to do with his parents and his brother, but I didn't ask. The turkey was greasy and the gravy pasty. I figured that wasn't why I felt ill. I drank a milkshake and watched Frank stare into his mixed vegetables, wishing the entire time he would hurry up so we could go home and do it, wishing the library wasn't closed for the long weekend.

The next day from a payphone I called my high school best friend Jen, back in Nashville studying law at Vandy after graduating from Rhodes, and told her everything. It was the Friday after Thanksgiving and my twenty-third birthday. Frank hadn't remembered and I didn't remind him. A card from my mom with a fifty-dollar check inside was the only thing that celebrated the day, and it'd come on Tuesday. School kids were roaming the dim winter streets of Ithaca throwing snowballs. One exploded against the phone booth glass in an eyelevel starburst while I wrote down the number of the women's clinic Jen found in the directory.

"Hold on," I told her, then cracked the accordion door and shrieked, "*Fuck you, you fucking little pussy!*" at the kid, maybe twelve years old, who'd thrown it. His friends laughed, but he looked like he was going to cry.

"What the hell is going on up there?" Jen asked.

"Bedlam. Anarchy. It gets dark at three o'clock. People go ape shit."

"Hey, isn't today your birthday?"

I read the clinic number back to her to make sure I had it right.

On the night of the last day of classes Frank drove me to the Syracuse airport. He hadn't finished a single paper all semester, and he was going to hole up in the apartment and write for the entire break. I did my best to feign sadness that he'd be alone on Christmas, but being trapped with him in the Datsun almost led me to abandon my plan to break up from afar and end it right there on Route 13.

He'd come up with a system to finish his papers that merged the kind of system he had for defrosting the freezer and the kind he had for appearing to have memorized all of Robert Browning, and he was explaining to me this new hybrid system in unrelenting detail. I considered directing him to pull over so we could have sex while parked on the snowy shoulder of the road, but I reminded myself I'd know as it was going on it was the last time. Wisely, after a tumble I hadn't thought of as our last as it happened, I decided that had been the last time, and so the last time was now one I could look back on with some amount of fondness, not one I'd moon over as it happened. It'd been good, that last time, I had to admit. Naked in bed, Frank was neither systematic robot nor lazy cheat. In the end I couldn't help myself and in the parking lot we fogged the windows recreating the night in DeWitt Park. I got on the plane wondering how in just five months I'd ended up so far away from that night.

As the little jet bumped south I tried to sleep, read magazines, regret the handjob in Syracuse—anything to keep from thinking about abortion. In Philadelphia I walked the concourses for the three-hour layover, trying to exhaust myself so I'd sleep on the flight to Nashville, but it didn't work. I was wide-awake and fretting the entire time.

I found Jen in the airport bar, playing Ms Pac-Man. Two plump businessmen with loose ties and askew comb-overs were leaning in and coaching her. It amazed me how Jen could suffer fools, and then it occurred to me what a gift Jen's patience was to a fool like me. She saw me out of the corner of her eye, drained her Coors Light, and blew the guys kisses as she walked away from the chirping machine.

She had a new Toyota Camry, a gift from a grandfather glad she'd thrown over the flute for law school. I stood in the parking lot stunned by the warm December night. I opened my coat and tipped back my head to look at weak stars and the winking lights of circling airplanes. "I *love* the *South*," I drawled.

"Hey, Blanche Dubois," Jen said, "get in the frickin' car."

On the road, I rolled down the window and stuck my head out into the thick air. An R.E.M. song was playing when I ducked back in. "I'm going to quit Cornell and come home."

"No, you're not," Jen told me, then said nothing else. We listened to Michael Stipe moan and keen.

I found the key hidden under the flowerpot on the back porch, snuck through the dark kitchen like I had on nights when I'd broken curfew, and used the guest bathroom on the first floor so the flush wouldn't wake my mother, asleep upstairs. There was blood on the paper when I wiped. I wasn't pregnant.

The next morning I woke to the smell of coffee and cardboard-tube sweet rolls and the sound of Jen and my mom talking in the kitchen. It was nine forty-five. My appointment at the clinic was at eleven, Jen had offered to drive me, but now there was no reason. I stared at the ceiling and marveled at the premature guilt I'd been suffering, guilt I thought I was too smart for.

"Hannah?" my mother called cheerily. "Time to wake up! Jennifer's here!"

She was smiling a tight smile when I came down in my pajamas. Jen was hiding behind a mug of coffee. It was easy to see she'd told my mom where we were going.

"I'm not pregnant."

"Well of course you're not!" my mother nearly sang.

Jen giggled, and when I heard her, laughter came up my throat so violently I gasped. It felt like it'd been months and months and months since I'd laughed, months of gorging on worry. Laughing felt like purging. I laughed until I was breathless, until tears blurred my vision.

Mom walked around the kitchen island and hugged me tightly. "It's okay, baby," she said into my hair.

I didn't talk about Frank while I sat on my mother's couch drinking box wine and dutifully watching college football as if my dad hadn't been dead for three years and would rush into the living room complaining if we changed the channel. I didn't talk about Frank while hanging out at Jen's apartment drinking thin beer and watching tapes of *Sixteen Candles* and *The Breakfast Club* and *Pretty in Pink*. I thought about Frank every waking, hung-over minute. I had dreams about dancing with him at the prom while he danced with the popular girl with big blonde hair while I watched him kick a field goal in overtime at homecoming while he and I sat under the bleachers making out and mocking the tool who kicked the field goal in overtime at homecoming.

On the morning of day six, December 31, I dialed my Ithaca number.

"Are you calling to break up with me?" he asked instead of saying hello.

I was taken aback. "How'd you know it was me?"

"Who else knows I'm here? Are you calling to break up?"

"No," I admitted, then felt I'd lost the upper hand. "Wait. Listen to me. My plan before I left Ithaca was to dump you. I was going to do it over the phone and tell you to get out before I got back. Then I decided I wasn't coming back, so I'd dump you and tell you to stay in the apartment if you wanted. Then I decided to come back and see if we can work things out."

"We can," he swore.

I waited for him to promise he'd never again lecture me on the right way to shelve books—alphabetically by author's name, divided by genre, hardcovers and paperbacks segregated. Instead he said, "I miss your dirty cereal bowl with the spoon stuck to the bottom and I miss the mole at the base of your spine and I miss the way you get so deep into whatever you're reading I have to say your name three times to get your attention."

Close enough to the promise I wanted, I decided, and cracked wise to keep from getting weepy: "I leave you alone for a few days and suddenly poetry's your fort."

"*Six* days, Han, six fucking days of silence. And the sun hasn't come out for a minute since you left. You're lucky I'm not out with Todd, hitting on the high school girls who work at Burger King."

"Just write your papers and stay away from Burger King and I'll be back soon," I told him, then added, "Happy New Year."

Frank's Spring semester schedule was Advanced Fiber Arts, an independent study on silence with a professor named Kierkegaard, and three thesis hours. I shook the printout at him. "Is this for real?" I'd been back in Ithaca for only a few hours and already the darkness and cold were making me testy.

Frank smiled. "I got them to count the independent study as American lit and the art class as an elective. The thesis hours bump me up to full-time so I keep getting my stipend."

I felt like a sucker. Flying north over landscapes of green, then brown, then dirty white, I'd accepted the fact I'd be spending another semester in classes that would be depressing and disappointing at best, infuriating and insulting at worst. I'd even forgiven my Tennessee professors. At least those old clowns worried their students might be smart enough to see through the pomposity they used to hide their laziness. No one seemed worried about that at Cornell. I'd convinced myself an Ivy League Ph.D. and all it promised was worth a few years of discomfort, but Frank had figured out how to earn the same degree working at the loom.

"An independent study on *silence?*" I was jealous even though I had no idea what that could mean. "With *Kierkegaard?*"

"He's a visiting art history professor from Denmark," Frank explained brightly. "He's writing a monograph about the first American photographer, a guy who lived in New Orleans in the 1840s. I met him at Denny's."

"I need some air."

"Wait. Okay, I know how to knit, that's why they allowed me into *Advanced* Fiber Arts. My grandma taught me right before she died, when I was about ten and she came to live with us, and I didn't tell you because I thought you might think it was sissy, but hold on." He ran to the closet and came back with a package that looked like a balloon made of newspaper. "Merry Christmas." When he dropped it into my arms, it burst and a banner five shades of purple unfurled across the floor.

He'd knitted me a scarf ten feet long and so soft it felt like it was made from teddy bear pelts. He wrapped it around my neck and shoulders and pulled me out into the frigid air, his gloved hand squeezing my mitten'd. The gray slab of sky had dimmed, Ithaca's winter version of twilight. Snow was falling. I loved the scarf and felt like crying. I'd assumed he'd be my ex-boyfriend by Christmas so I hadn't gotten him anything, then I'd forgotten to get him something after the hubbub of not being pregnant and not breaking up. He was smiling, almost skipping. The snow looked as if it were pouring from the streetlights.

We rounded the corner and came upon a yard sale, a bizarre sight in the snow and the dark. Beside a card table stacked with toys a teenaged boy stood imploring a man who appeared to be his father—same nose, albeit crooked, same chin, albeit beefier.

"Take what you want," the man told Frank when we stopped to browse.

"Excuse me?" Frank said.

"Dumbfuck here stole his sister's allowance to buy weed, so take what you want."

The kid looked away.

"I like your scarf," the man told me.

I pointed proudly to Frank. "He made it for me."

"You knit?" the guy said incredulously, eyebrows rising.

I wished I'd said it was a gift. Being thoughtful wasn't fruity. Frank picked up a toy video camera from the table.

"His grandmother taught him."

The man looked like he was reconsidering giving his child's things to Frank.

"Just say no," Frank scolded the kid, then pulled me along the sidewalk, back toward the apartment. Already the footprints we'd made were filling with snow. Soon they'd be gone.

In the cold bedroom, Frank slowly took off my clothes, even my socks, and then draped the impossibly soft scarf around my neck and looped a half hitch under my chin. It hung over my breasts, rubbed my knees, pooled on the tops of my bare feet. I shivered from lust. I wanted to do it wearing the scarf. Frank knelt and began wrapping me in the scarf and I understood this was its purpose and I didn't feel so bad about not getting him a Christmas gift.

In the mirror on the back of the closet door I saw myself tied up in purple rope, lover supplicating before me. Still on his knees, Frank looked over his shoulder at the mirror. His reflected eyes widened when I lifted my hand from where it rested atop his head and stuck my fingers into the yarn between my legs. He frantically fumbled with the buckle of his belt.

13

I had to imagine dawn each dark morning. Around six every evening I tried to recall the way winter sunlight in Tennessee slowly changed as dusk fell. The colorless landscape I trudged through between pretend sunrise and make-believe sunset made me feel like I was trapped inside the little black-and-white TV on which Frank watched basketball. Even tropical beaches were gray on its screen. In the mirror, my face looked bloodless as the face of the local weatherman who predicted more sunless cold.

"How can you stand it?" I asked in the middle of a Celtics-Cavaliers game.

Frank turned away from a monochromatic beer commercial as if I'd caught him staring at a woman in the street. "Sorry—what?"

"The sun doesn't shine. Ever."

He shrugged. "I'm from Cleveland. At least it doesn't stink here."

The halls of the English department were slick with filthy water that'd once been filthy snow. Classrooms were gloomy, as if the frozen wiring couldn't carry enough wattage to light fully the bulbs. I worried something was wrong with my brain when again and again I found myself in the middle of making a point and forgetting what that point was—then I noticed the confused looks on the faces of Joanie, Nat, Sam, and Todd whenever they spoke, and I felt less panicked. Professor Caldweel, who taught early American literature, would sometimes abruptly stop lecturing and sit blinking, then demand, "Who's your favorite Mather?"

Pat Caldweel's seminar was the first class at Cornell I liked. She was a wonderfully weird little woman with perfect teeth and eyes the same steel gray as the long braid she wore to her waist. "If no one picks Increase, I'm going to be royally pissed," she told us each time she asked for our votes on the Mathers. She clearly loved the books she had us read—Jefferson's *Notes on the State of Virginia,* Crevecoeur's *Letters from an American Farmer*—and quoted long sections of them from memory. I couldn't remember much of what was said between one and four o'clock on Tuesdays, perhaps because of the wine I drank from five to whenever with Joanie and Nat and Sam in the kitchen of the little house Nat and Sam shared, perhaps because I was overjoyed to be making friends with women who joked about Ben Franklin and *Gilligan's Island,* but even in my cups I remembered feeling exhilarated from the challenge of having to keep up with Pat Caldweel, a thrill keen enough to cut through the weak light of those Upstate winter days.

Bed and books, bed and books, bed and books—so the dim, frozen months passed. I wasn't trying to silence Frank when I suggested he tie me up with the scarf, or I tie him, or we bind ourselves together. (After a sweaty assignation before or between or after classes, I wrapped it around my neck and face and headed out into the cold.) He abandoned most of his systems, kept quiet about those he didn't. I decided there was nothing wrong with having my underwear laundered, folded, and put away, nothing wrong with having my dirty coffee cup disappear from the desk and reappear, clean, in the cabinet.

I wasn't trying to avoid Frank when I went to my library carrel and read with delight women's Indian captivity narratives: *A True History of the Captivity and Restoration of Mrs. Mary Rowlandson. God's Mercy Surrounding Man's Cruelty,*

Exemplified in the Captivity and Redemption of Elizabeth Hanson, Wife of John Hanson. A Genuine and Correct Account of the Captivity, Sufferings and Deliverance of Mrs. Jemima Howe. They were tough Puritans. The Indians killed their kids, their sisters, their mothers-in-law. Able-bodied husbands and uncles were usually not at home when the raids occurred, and if they were, they were quickly dispatched. The women's tales were blunt and plain; "a suckling Child they knock'd on the head" was a frequent detail. I liked the simple force of their stories: this horror happened, then this horror, then this horror, then the Indians sold me to the French, who tried to make me convert to Papism, and then the French ransomed me back to the English, and now I'm telling you about it, Dear Christian Reader. The women spent a lot of time cold and trudging through snow. I could relate. Sometimes, given the chance, they killed their captivators and took their scalps to collect bounty.

My favorite was Sarah Weed's *The Goodness and Soveraignty of God.* On its surface Goody Weed's story was much like the hundreds of other captivity narratives written and published in New England in the late seventeenth and early eighteenth centuries. Its plot was not unusual—kidnapped during a raid, marched through the woods in wintertime, made to eat odd food and witness heathen dancing, ransomed back to her in-laws by the French—and its mix of anthropological detail, melodrama, and Biblical free association wasn't novel. What made *The Goodness and Soveraignty of God* different and wonderful was that Sarah Weed's husband Samuel was also taken captive and Sarah was not pleased to have his company. On the first page, in the middle of the requisite descriptions of the firing of the barns and the tomahawking of the old men, Sarah Weed describes for Dear Christian Reader how Samuel, wise to the ways of the marauders, strips off his clothes and puts on a dress. Suckling children are knock'd on the head, and Sarah and Samuel are led into the woods, Sarah judging, "Samuel was a plain and not handsome man, but as a bonnet'd Goodwife, he was monstrous."

Sarah Weed thanks God for her suffering, as all the captives do (reading their tales I quickly learned Psalm 119, verse 71: "It is good for me that I have been afflicted; that I might learn thy statutes"), including the suffering Samuel causes her—a beating when he steals groundnuts (a native legume with an edible tuber, I figured out) and claims Sarah ate them, a beating they both receive when his crying keeps the camp awake. Three days into the journey Samuel is found out and knock'd on the head. "The Coward was betray'd by his Beard only moments before I was driven to betray him," Sarah remarks. "The day following was quiet and filled with lovely Sunlight." She never again mentions her husband.

Sarah Weed paid to have the first edition of *The Goodness and Soveraignty of God* published, and while its success was modest in comparison to other narratives, the seventy-two copies she boasts of selling in a letter to a Provincetown friend appear to have been enough to interest a Boston printer named Ezekiel Breech who edited and printed the second edition—in which Samuel Weed is killed during the raid whilst valiantly defending his wife and barns. Throughout the text Sarah's denigrations of her husband are replaced with lamentations about his death.

I looked for criticism that noted this change and found none. A little research made it clear Cornell's rare book library had what may have been the only remaining copy of the first edition. The single article that mentioned *The Goodness and Soveraignty of God* was about Ezekiel Breech and the history of publishing in Boston in the eighteenth century. In it Sarah Weed's narrative is dismissed in an endnote: "Breech reprinted a number of works originally privately published by their authors, including knock-offs of popular titles. In 1708 an advertisement boasts of a pamphlet entitled *The Goodness and Soveraignty of God* that appears to be little more than a secondhand version of *A True History of the Captivity and Restoration of Mrs. Mary Rowlandson.*"

I wrote an essay about the role men played in the production of the narratives—as editors, printers, and, in several instances, as writers who crafted the most sanctimonious captivity tales from reports offered by former captives, if they didn't simply invent them. I used the two versions of Sarah Weed's narrative as the central example of how those men continually sought to alter the stories of women held captive by Indians into propaganda beneficial to their own commercial, racial, religious, and gender agendas. Pat Caldweel gave me an A and suggested at the end of three single-spaced pages of typed praise stapled to the paper that I consider captivity narratives and the history of the book in early America as the focus of my dissertation. I clutched the essay as gleefully as I'd once in high school clutched the note from Wes Owen asking if I wanted to go steady.

14

One day near the end of April as I walked across campus, a breeze warm as breath tickled my ear, and when I spun around, expecting Frank behind me, I found instead spring-time.

15

"I finished my silence independent study," Frank told me the day after the semester ended.

"Can I read it—silently?"

He nodded at my joke, but didn't smile, and I felt lame.

"Okay, here's the thing, it's movies."

"It's about silent movies?" I was confused.

"No, *it is* movies. I made movies. About silence."

"I'm confused."

"Remember when that guy was giving away his kid's stuff because the kid stole his sister's money to buy pot? I used that camera."

I grinned. "The night you gave me the scarf."

Frank nodded, then fetched the camera from the closet, attached it to a wire on the back of the little black-and-white I'd never noticed, popped in what looked like an audiocassette, and pushed *play*.

The first film was of a streetlamp haloed by snow. Frank said nothing. The only sound in the room was the barely audible screech of the tape's spools spinning inside the camera. The film was five minutes long and just that one shot: snow fluttering in the glow like moths would flutter there on a summer night.

The next tape was of icicles against a background of smudged gray sky. I waited for a droplet to grow on the tip of one, hang, fall, but it wasn't an educational film about the changing seasons; it was a record of winter's silence.

Five black-and-white minutes of a tabby cat, asleep behind a window begrimed on one side by winter and on the other by the cat's nose.

Five black-and-white minutes of a paperback romance novel in a puddle of slush, its embossed cover torn, its pulp pages imperceptibly fattening as they absorb gritty half-melted snow.

Five black-and-white minutes of a single mistimed cherry blossom, shellacked in ice.

Each was a fragment of silence, not a noisy moment made mute for effect, and I felt calm, like I'd had a glass of wine while watching the dancing snow, the sleeping cat, the frozen flower.

Frank started the last tape and I saw myself naked and asleep on top of the blankets, the scarf knotted around one ankle. I was covered in shadows thrown by sunlight that found its way through the dome of clouds for a moment one winter afternoon while I dozed. The shadows moved when a draft leaked through the frame of the old window and touched the curtain. I looked like I was underwater. Watching was like dreaming.

I looked up at Frank and tried to say *I love you* but it came out "You love me." He nodded, his expression serious. "I mean *I love you*." Still serious, he nodded again.

I understood the strange grin Kierkegaard had given me the day I ran into him in the library, and I felt myself blushing in retrospective embarrassment. The tape ended and the image froze and the shadows were fixed on me like tattoos.

"Let's get married."

He looked startled, then sighed. "Don't joke."

"Who's joking? Let's get married."

16

Joanie and Nat cornered me in the English department toilet when I went to campus to turn in some overdue library books and check my mailbox.

"You don't have to do this," Nat said. Joanie nodded.

I was ruminating about my library fines—almost seventy-five dollars, all for books I'd checked out for Frank—and at first thought they were telling me I didn't have to pay.

"We'll go with you to the clinic," Joanie said in a soothing voice. "It's okay."

"I'm not getting married because I'm pregnant."

They cut their eyes at each other. "You don't have to have the baby—or you can have it without getting married." Joanie's soothing tone curdled into condescension. "This isn't Kentucky."

"I'm from Tennessee," I corrected. "And I'm not an ignorant hick who's gotten herself knocked up." I slammed a stall door behind myself and remembered how Joanie had snorted at me the first time we met. I'd been a fool to believe she'd become my friend.

When I walked into the mailroom, Joanie was there with a professor named Maude Reynolds who said, "Tell me you're not changing your name."

Joanie pretended to read a flyer tacked above the Xerox machine.

"From Guttentag to Doyle? You bet I am."

Reynolds shook her head. "You disappoint me, *Mrs. Doyle.*"

As I walked out of Goldwin Smith I considered the jerk professors at UT, snorting Joanie and the other backup singers, professors Presley, Reynolds, et al. I remembered the way my father closed his eyes and touched his fingertips to his temples when he told my mother about another typo-filled memo from his vice principal regarding faculty parking, or student dress code enforcement, or a mandatory unpaid Saturday seminar on Satanism and heavy metal music led by a local evangelical minister.

"I want respect," I said to a guy cutting the grass. He smiled and waved, my voice lost in the buzz of his mower's motor.

17

June in Upstate New York was mild as Tennessee spring, and I was happy to be reminded of those first days in Ithaca I'd spent wandering with Kree, the days before long winter and mercurial April and May—warm and sunny one morning, cold and gray the next. Frank and I were the only people I knew who stayed in town after the semester ended. I felt grown-up and poor. Todd and Joanie and the rest were at their parents' summer homes in Maine or on Cape Cod or Martha's Vineyard.

The roofer Frank worked for the previous summer hired him again, this time at twice what he'd paid before when he learned Frank had a commercial driver's license and knew how to operate a forklift. I found an ad for full-time temporary office work on a bulletin board at the co-op grocery. The next Monday I followed the flyer's instructions and showed up at eight a.m. at low, gray building on a cul-de-sac behind City Hall. The harried woman who answered the door asked through the glass, "Do you know the alphabet?"

"I'm getting a Ph.D. in English at Cornell."

She unlocked the door. "So you can type?"

The office was a maze of deserted cubicles. She led me to one in which an overexposed picture of a family fishing off a dock was tacked to the fabric wall and a half-empty bottle of Diet Coke stood beside a dead potted plant. Stacks of files leaned off the desk's edge.

"Can you start today?" the woman asked before she even told me what the job entailed.

For a week I sorted files into storage boxes. When I opened one to try to figure out what'd once gone on in the office, I was stymied by technical jargon and long lists of coordinates recorded in latitude and longitude. On Friday afternoon the woman—Nancy—brought me a thick folder and explained, "You're in charge of payroll." Before she left she went from cube to cube with a grocery bag, looting them of staplers and calculators and rulers and hole punches.

That left just me and the guy with the key to the office, Sebastian, who was taking classes to become a court reporter. His job was to answer the phone and refuse delivery of packages from UPS and FedEx; he let every call go to voicemail and put a sign on the door; in one cubicle he napped, in another he did yoga, in a third he read pamphlets with beatific bearded men on their covers. It took me another week to find the last of the files to pack up. By the middle of June there was no more work. We kept coming to the office every day, waiting for someone to tell us to stop. Our paychecks appeared on my desk each Friday morning.

One day I listened to Sebastian mumbling an echo of the taped court proceedings he listened to on his Walkman and practiced transcribing on his stenotype machine. He was two cubicles away, and when I asked him a question and figured out he couldn't hear me, I called Jen long distance on the office phone and left a message on her machine telling her Frank and I had decided to get married in New Orleans on July 15 and I hoped she'd be able to be there, then called her back and left a second message telling her I wasn't pregnant, then called again to ask if she remembered our senior-year high school band trip when the skanky guy with a mustache he'd draw on with a Sharpie hit on us on Bourbon Street.

New Orleans was neutral and exotic. Frank had never been. I told him about Mardi Gras and Jazz Fest, didn't mention who I'd been with catching beads and dancing to Dr. John.

On the morning of June 30 I showed up and found Sebastian riding his bike in circles around the empty parking lot.

"Someone changed the locks," he told me. "These were taped to the door." He handed me an envelope and I opened it to find a check and a pink slip. "I didn't know pink slips were really pink," he said, and then rode off without a good-bye.

18

Frank and I flew to New Orleans and checked into a hotel in the French Quarter. The suite, a gift from my mom, was a tiny old Creole cottage that'd been annexed by the hotel. The sitting room's windows afforded a view of the shoulders and heads of pedestrians on Toulouse Street. A narrow hallway led from the front room to a tiny kitchen, the bathroom, and a bedroom with French doors that opened onto a courtyard with a fountain and banana trees.

I had to stand on a chair to hook the hanger holding my dress over a blade of the front room's ceiling fan because its short train was too long for the closet's rod. Frank found a *Dukes of Hazzard* rerun on a cable station I'd never heard of and stretched out on the couch to watch Bo and Luke jump the General Lee over dry creek beds.

Up on the chair, I worried the dress was too white, too lacy, altogether too much for a ceremony that would take place the next afternoon in the little courtyard right outside the bedroom, a ceremony presided over by a Justice of the Peace and attended only by my mother and Jen. I wondered if I could find something simpler in a dress shop in the Quarter, if I could find a shop still open—it was already six. I didn't want to wait until morning to try to buy a replacement.

"Wow." Frank looked up at me and at the dress, smiling. "You're going to look fantastic in that." On the TV, Daisy Duke was serving beer to grinning hicks at the Boar's Nest. "Is it bad luck for me to see the dress?"

"Not unless I'm in it."

He nodded. "I feel lucky when you're out of your dress."

I led Frank along Orleans Avenue, down Pirate's Alley, and through Jackson Square. My love for the Quarter was magnified by his awe. He took pictures of iron railings, faded signs advertising extinct soda pop, the ornate tops of water meter covers, Jesus in the garden behind the St. Louis cathedral, a guy playing a sousaphone. At Café du Monde I taught him how to eat beignets without covering his shirt with powdered sugar or blowing it onto me. Frank took a picture of me sipping coffee and watching tourists walk past. I had to remind myself I was one of them. My affection for the city made me feel my connection to it was deeper than any connection felt by the flat-voiced Midwesterners who sat at the next table mopping their necks with paper napkins and wondering loudly how anyone could drink *coffee* when it was so *darn hot*. I loved the heat, the coffee, the smell of the river. I wasn't ignorant of New Orleans' indiscriminate seduction, the way it makes everyone feel they alone understand its complexities, they alone can see past the T-shirt shops selling out-of-season Mardi Gras beads and rubber crawfish and teeny gift bottles of hot sauce to an authentic secret world in which they fit in like they fit in nowhere else. Even the embarrassed teenaged brother and sister sitting with their complaining parents had in their downcast eyes a look I recognized—vaguely guilty, hazily afraid. I wanted to tell them being lured by a seducer as overwhelming, strange, and beautiful as New Orleans was nothing to be ashamed of, nothing to fear.

We ate a hundred-dollar early dinner with a fifty-dollar bottle of red—unheard of extravagance for us—then wandered the Quarter drinking Hand Grenades while the sun dimmed and the neon came on.

When Frank boasted we were getting married the next day, the bartender at Tropical Isle served me my second

Hand Grenade in a huge green plastic penis with a straw stuck in its tip. I was too drunk to be offended.

"Also," the guy said, and from a box behind the bar fetched me a Halloween-costume bride's veil, a swatch of white toile glued to a plastic hairband. "Congratulations."

We stood in the middle of Bourbon Street and watched through the open door of a strip club a woman wearing only red patent-leather boots. I sipped from the penis and adjusted my veil. I was buzzed on booze and Kool-Aid and having a great time. Frank pointed to the stripper. She'd dropped into a squat facing us.

"I like her shoes," he said.

None of the streetlights were on. Only neon beer signs lit the sidewalks when I tried to lead Frank to the river. Off Bourbon it was spooky.

"Why's it so dark?" Frank asked the bartender in an Irish dive we happened upon. A single candle was guttering on the bar.

"Termites."

"Excuse me?" I didn't think I was that drunk.

She clicked on a paper lantern, and as soon as the bulb inside was lit, a swarm of bugs filled the white globe and rattled frantically against the rice paper.

"That's fucked up," Frank proclaimed into his plastic cup of beer.

We followed a boat horn's lowing to the levee and watched the greasy Mississippi undulating in the darkness. Off to the left, a tugboat took the bend in the river. Frank tipped my head back with a finger under my chin and kissed me so fiercely I stumbled and saw sparks behind my eyelids. He hugged me hard to keep me on my feet. I was gasping when he let go. He dropped to his knees, ducked his head up under my skirt, and kissed the crotch of the purple lace panties I'd bought for the trip. My knees were loose from booze and lust.

"I don't want to do it here."

"Okay," he said from underneath my skirt. He sounded disappointed.

"But I do want to do it," I clarified. "Just not here."

We nearly ran back to Toulouse.

Frank fell over the threshold after he unlocked the door. "What just happened?" he asked from the floor.

I looked into the dark room, saw a headless ghost hovering, and screamed.

Frank popped up and cocked his fists. "What just happened?"

"The dress. It's the dress."

Frank closed the door, grabbed my arm, and pulled me through the suite to the bedroom. We were too drunk to think to turn off the bedside lamp. Frank kissed my neck and ears and eyelids, covered my face with the costume veil, wiggled down to the foot of the bed, and put his head between my legs. I let my head loll on the pillow and through the veil I saw dirty water pouring under the French doors. I flipped the veil up and saw it was not a flood, but thousands and thousands of termites.

"Stop!" I barked. "Bugs!"

Later he told me he'd thought I was confessing to having crabs, which would've been an admission of infidelity—but then he saw the swarm covering the white slip of the pillow we'd kicked off the bed.

He hissed, "Shit, shit, shit" as he ran to the bathroom and came back with wet towels he stuffed across the bottoms of the doors.

I twisted off the light and felt something on my foot and sobbed, "I can't sleep here!"

"Sofa bed in the other room." Frank was turning off every light, covering the clock's glowing numbers with a sock, the fire alarm's red eye with my panties, the VCR's flashing noon or midnight with his boxers.

"Carry me?"

He lifted me from the bed and lugged me down the short hallway into the other room. I stood on top of two couch cushions while he unfolded the groaning hide-a-bed. Dim light from Toulouse made it possible to see his outline. Above the bed my luminous dress moved in the dark. "Get my shoes?"

"Your shoes?"

"I'm drunk and I'm naked and my honeymoon suite is infested by a swarm of termites and I want to hold my wedding shoes up to my wedding dress, okay?"

Frank sighed. "Okay."

I heard him feel his way down the unlit hall to the closet, then search in the dark for the shoebox. I climbed up onto the bed. My eyes were level with the waist of the dress. When I touched it, I was a little surprised it was real. I didn't know he was back until he spoke.

"It's dark," he apologized. "I don't think you'll be able to see much."

I reached toward his voice and found the shoes and held up the satin pumps and saw a ghost's dim feet below the vague hem of a ghost's dress.

I heard the springs of the foldout when Frank lay down and shifted around, searching for a comfortable spot on the thin mattress upon which I still stood.

I was not so drunk I didn't know every bride spent the final hours before she wed worrying, but termites were a dangerous omen. They ruined houses and houses were the universal symbol of happy marriages.

Frank reached out and touched my foot. "What're you doing up there?"

"The dress." I didn't want to tell him I was convinced termites were bad luck, and therefore our marriage was doomed before it began. "The shoes." I looked down and saw only the shape of naked Frank, a shade darker than the white sheet, but I knew the look he was giving me—raised eyebrows, crooked puzzled smile—and I decided the ability to see in the dark the loving, puzzled face of my fiancé was proof I was meant to be with him, termites notwithstanding.

19

My head hurt so badly it woke me up. Sunlight blasted the room and above me the dress floated in the brilliance, shivering in the AC's breeze. Beside me Frank lay with his ankles crossed and his arms out as if he'd been nailed to the bed, one of my shoes above his head in lieu of halo. I still wore the other. I vaguely recalled having sex for a very long time. His cheeks, rough with stubble, had scraped the insides of my thighs. I regarded the pillows and the sight of them awakened in my mind secret amiable memories.

Someone was knocking at the courtyard door. Still more than a little drunk, I got up, kicked off my shoe, and made my unsteady way from the front room to the bedroom. I paused to see if the sight of the toilet might convince my stomach to give up some poison, but it was too late for puking. What I really needed to do was pee.

"Hold on," I shouted. My voice was like a hammer between my eyes. I had to lean against the bathroom doorframe until my head stopped spinning.

"Hannah," my mother called. "It's us."

I was afraid termites were hiding in the clothes on the floor, so I took the wadded sheet off the bed, shook it, and wrapped myself in it.

When I opened the door, my mother's smile fell and Jen's rose. I looked over my shoulder and saw what they saw: purple panties dangling from the smoke alarm; green plastic penis, erect but half-empty of booze, on the bedside table; veil in the epicenter of the bed.

I wanted to cry when Mom took one more look into the room and excused herself to go and see if the cake had arrived.

Jen stepped in and closed the door. "She's freaking because her baby's getting married and your dad's not here. She's been weepy and cranky since we left Nashville." She hugged me. "You stink. Take a shower, then we'll get some coffee."

I nodded. "Frank's asleep. In the other room."

"I promise I'll keep it down." She picked up the remote and turned on the bedroom TV. Boss Hogg was abusing Roscoe.

I sat in the tub under the shower and almost fell asleep. When I thought about coffee, I retched. When I thought about wedding cake, I retched. Even thinking about *Dukes of Hazzard* made me dry heave. I washed my hair and hoped I'd fallen and hit my head the night before. It didn't seem possible it could hurt so badly just from booze, but I couldn't find a lump.

The curtain zipped open and Jen stood above me, laughing. I crossed my arms over my chest, confused and embarrassed.

"Your beau woke up," she said. "I didn't hear him coming and he didn't know I was in the room." She cranked off the water and tossed me a towel. "So now I've seen the groom and the bride naked, which I think is a New Orleans tradition."

I found Frank in the hide-a-bed with the covers pulled up to his chin. "You okay?"

"Sorry, Frank," Jen yelled from the other room.

"That's Jen."

"She introduced herself when I walked into the room wearing nothing but a hangover."

I tried not to laugh and failed, then had to hold my head to keep it from splitting open. "She thinks you're cute."

Frank pulled the sheet up over his face. "Bring me coffee—bring me big coffee, please."

We went to a patisserie on Charters where Jen ordered black coffee and brioche for me, espresso for herself. We sat under an umbrella in the courtyard. The first sip of dark roast made me spit up a mouthful of thin gray-green bile into a potted palm.

"Jesus, Han, how much did you have last night?"

I stuffed brioche into my mouth, hoping it would sop up the dregs of the booze roiling in my gut. I washed it down with coffee and it stayed down, a good sign. "All I remember is there was a point when I thought, *it's not a good idea to keep drinking this,* then I kept drinking it, and then everything gets wavy."

I took another big bite and Jen grinned foolishly while I chewed. "What?" I asked with my mouth full.

Jen kept grinning. "I knew you when you had your first crush, when you had your first kiss, when you had to look up 'fellatio' after Wes suggested it in a note he left in your locker."

I drained my cup. "Good old Wes. Where would I be without his suggestions?"

"Seriously, Han, doesn't this seem hard to believe?" Jen gestured to the blue sky above. "I mean, what if I told you I'd fallen in love with someone and I was getting married?"

The coffee and bread were clearing my head. "That would freak me out."

Jen nodded. "Why?"

I needed more French roast and another brioche, not be coached through a conversation. I was getting weepy as I sobered. "Because, I don't know, like you said, we've known each other for a long time."

"We have, but here's what I think: Since we went away to college and stopped being around each other all the time, we think of each other as the person we knew back in high school. I think of you as the chick from marching band who talked me into helping you shoplift *The Joy of Sex* from Walden Books so we could figure out what the hell Wes and the other boys were talking about, and you think of me as the lookout for that crime, not as the law student who might have a fiancé. That's why having Frank saunter into the room like an illustration from *The Joy of Sex* come to life was mind-bending."

My forehead felt like it was inflating, worry expanding like a migraine. "Oh shit, he doesn't look like one of those guys, does he?"

"It's okay. He looks a little like the hot one, not the Charles Manson one."

I laughed, but stopped when my eyeballs felt like they were pulsing.

When we got back to the hotel, we found Frank and my mother sitting on the couch, holding hands. It looked like they'd been crying. I held a cup of coffee out to Frank and when he took it with his left hand I tried to remember in which hand he held a pen.

"Dot and I were talking about my parents."

"And about your dad," my mother added.

"And my brother." Frank took a long swallow of coffee and shuddered.

I nodded. He never talked about his family. Aside from staring silently into his plate the Thanksgiving we went to Denny's and acting oddly depressed and obsessed when a Browns or Indians or Cavaliers game was on TV, it was as if they'd never been in the car crash he mentioned just once. I felt slightly betrayed, then felt foolish for feeling so. People told mothers things they didn't tell their lovers, even if the aforesaid mother was the mother of the lover. My head hurt.

"Give me a sip of that coffee," I told Frank.

"Jennifer," my mother said, "I think we should go."

"I'll be back in an hour to help you get dressed," Jen told me.

After they left I went to the bathroom and then peeked into the bedroom. The bed was made and there was no sign of the obscene cup or my underwear. When I'd washed my hands, there were no new towels or hand soaps. The maid hadn't come; Frank had cleaned up.

He was sitting on the couch with his head thrown back and his eyes closed and tongue stuck out. He looked like he'd died after I left the room.

"You okay?"

"Coffee burned my tongue." He opened his eyes and lifted his head. "You feeling rough?"

"What did you talk about with my mom?"

Frank shrugged. "She told me she wished your dad could've met me, I told her I wished my mom and dad and brother could've met you, and then she started crying, and then I started crying."

I felt like crying, too. "You wish your mom could've met me?"

"Come here." He held open his arms. I sat in his lap and he hugged me. "Of course I wish my mom could've met you, and my dad and Harmon."

He'd never said his brother's name before. "Harmon," I repeated.

"A great uncle. I got off easy with Franklin—my grand-father's name."

Jen painted my lids with pale lilac shadow, curled my lashes, powdered my nose, pretended to stumble over a lecture on the birds and the bees and wedding nights that left us laughing so hard I smeared my makeup and she had to start over.

She twisted my hair into a bun at the nape of my neck. "This needs something," she said, and left me sitting on the couch, looking at my done-up face in a mirror in an antiqued frame.

"Harmon," I said to my reflection. The surprise I'd felt when Frank told me he wished his brother could've met me had been downright old-fashioned, a shock like the one naïve brides got in dirty jokes. There were things about Frank I thought I knew, but I didn't, things I now understood I'd find out about in flashes over the otherwise lazy passage of years of married life, not during the manic first months.

"I stole this baby's breath from a arrangement in the lobby," Jen bragged when she came back. She stuck the flower into my hair, then pulled it out and stuck it in again at a different angle.

"Crap," I said. "I forgot to order a bouquet."

"You want me to go steal more flowers?" Jen plugged in the iron and unfolded the board.

Someone knocked on the courtyard door and I went to answer, assuming it was my mother or Frank. Instead it was the concierge, an older black guy in a red jacket with gold braid and admiral's epaulets who'd earlier directed us to the coffee shop.

"Saw that other girl take some flowers and figured you could use these." From behind his back he produced a huge bouquet of white roses: I wished for flowers and they appeared.

"Two dozen. Woman was long gone by the time her man sent her these," he explained. "Hate to see them go to waste."

"Wow, thanks." I held the heavy flowers with both hands.

Jen's arm came from under my elbow, a third hand with a twenty-dollar bill in its fingers.

"Too kind," the bellman said as he folded the money into his pocket.

❀

The wedding was quick. The Justice of the Peace was a perfect caricature: seersucker suit, shock of white hair, breath sweet with bourbon, Foghorn Leghorn drawl. "We are gathered in the sight of God," he began. I held a dozen perfect roses and a thirteenth was pinned to Frank's lapel. *Harmon* echoed in my head, dulling the ache. It was a code word, a promise, maybe the name of a child I might someday have, someday, maybe. The fountain plashed and I heard parrots cawing nearby. "You may kiss the bride," the justice said, and Frank did.

I changed into the yellow sundress I'd worn to the party in Ithaca where we became a public couple, and we all went to dinner at Antoine's. The tiled room was brightly lit and loud with the noise of forks and knives and happy voices. Oysters Rockefeller, gumbo, Chateaubriand for the bride and groom, creamed spinach, *pommes de terre soufflés,* baked Alaska—if there was a perfect menu to erase a hangover, this was it. Frank and I played footsie and tried to keep straight faces while we split a cold bottle of hair-of-the-dog white. There were toasts and counter-toasts. My headache was gone and between courses I said a silent prayer of thanks for all the blessings I'd received: Frank, Mom, Jen, the food, the flowers, New Orleans.

After coffee we stood on the sidewalk, stunned by meat and wine and ice cream, listening to a tugboat blowing its horn on the river just blocks away. I'm married, I realized, astonished.

Frank and Jen and Mom laughed.

"What?"

"You said that out loud," my mother told me.

When Frank kissed me, I felt the slow soothing beat of my heart quicken.

20

On Fridays Joanie and Nat and Sam went to the Six Mile Creek swimming hole, back in the woods, where everyone swam naked, and the first Friday we were back from New Orleans, I told Frank I wanted to go.

"Sure you wouldn't rather Buttermilk? I like Buttermilk."

The pool at the base of Buttermilk Falls had lifeguards and ropes with red and white floats to keep little kids away from the deep. Nudity wasn't allowed. Frank was trying to be nice. He knew I always refused invitations to Six Mile.

"Too many fat families picnicking and teenagers trying to hook up at Buttermilk." I hadn't told him Joanie and Nat offered to take me to the clinic and refused to believe I wasn't getting married because I was pregnant, and I didn't care to admit I wanted to show off a flat stomach and a hot husband more than I wanted to beat the mild heat.

Joanie and Todd were in the middle of the pool, up to their chins in water, kissing, when we came out of the woods. Joanie had her hands over Todd's ears like she was trying to keep him from hearing a secret. Through the clear water I saw the pale fish of his erection.

"Howdy," Frank said, then unbuckled his belt and dropped his cutoffs.

Joanie pushed Todd away. "Hey, Frank. Hey, Hannah. Hey."

I could feel my smile stretching my face. "Where're Nat and Sam?"

"Beer run," Todd said in a bored voice. He crossed his hands in front of his crotch and feigned disinterest as Joanie half-swam, half-walked away from him. "How's married life?" He made *married life* sound like *stomach flu.*

"Todd, my man, I cannot thank you enough for insulting Hannah." Frank stuck his foot into the water. "Chilly." He looked over his shoulder gave me a conspiratorial smirk. "I don't think she would've liked me as much if you hadn't given me the chance to defend her honor."

Joanie wouldn't meet my eye, even when I made myself stop grinning.

Todd giggled in falsetto and I realized he was high. On the opposite side of the swimming hole a one-hitter was nested on a sandwich bag of weed. I watched Joanie fanning her arms to keep her head above water even though she was standing on the bottom and bending her knees, and I knew she too was loaded.

The swimming hole was the result of a rocky bottleneck that squeezed the creek and backed up water into a round pond twenty feet across and four feet deep. Trees grew to the very edge of the pool and were reflected in it. Todd and Joanie and Frank looked like they were levitating in foliage.

I felt my ears burn when I pulled my shirt over my head. I watched my shorts and underwear cover the tops of my feet, then stepped out of them and kept my eyes on the ground. I hoped Joanie could tell I wasn't sucking in my gut or slouching to disguise the beginnings of a baby bump. Up to my ankles in cold water, I peeked and saw her looking up at the trees and Todd peering down at the rocky bottom—good hot tub manners. Only Frank watched me. He wore a blissful smile. "Water's fine, wifey," he said, patting the surface beside him.

Sam and Nat arrived with a case of High Life tallboys. A shelf of rock along one side of the pool was a perfect bench and we sat armpit-deep, hip-to-hip, me-Frank-Joanie-Todd-Sam-Nat, passing the pipe. Soon we were all buzzed on Miller and Todd's dope and laughing as Frank told the story of the termites coming under the door in New Orleans—minus the detail he was going down on me when the bugs invaded.

I saw the women sneaking sidelong glances at each other and at Frank and Todd, and Todd openly eyeing the women, and felt I'd been given permission. Joanie was plump and pale-skinned. Blonde Nat's tan lines made her small breasts look bigger. Sam had a bright pink six-inch scar under her bellybutton that resembled a zipper, and at one end of it was tattooed a matching-scale YKK pull. I looked down at myself and wondered what they saw when they peeked at me: proof my red hair was authentic, proof I hadn't lied when I said I wasn't pregnant, proof I needed to go to the rec center to tone my flabby ass. I slyly checked out Todd to make myself feel better. A thick stripe of dark hair ran from nipple to nipple and down over his bulbous belly to his navel—T for Todd. His penis had shrunk to the size of his thumb. I pretended to scratch my knee and looked between Frank's legs to see if the cold water did that to all men. It didn't.

We drank beer and told silly stories and laughed, but even as I was having fun and forgiving the women who'd hurt my feelings, I knew we'd climb from the water as soon as the sun began to dim and the air to cool, look away from each other, shiver as we dressed, silently walk the path through the woods to the road, and leave in three cars, Frank and I in the Datsun, Nat and Sam in their VW camper, Joanie and Todd in his Volvo. The faint connection between the six of us was strong for the afternoon because we were all naked, all looped on cheap beer and trust-fund weed, because summer was ending and soon we'd spend our days in crowds in classrooms, alone in library carrels, or paired up in bed or on the couch watching reruns.

21

On the last day of August I woke to the ping and hiss of the radiator. Ithaca's lovely, limited summer was over and it was time to go back to school.

I was registered for seminars on Spenser, Modernist British poetry, and bibliography and methods. Frank had managed another schedule that made me jealous and disappointed in Cornell and in him: an undergraduate class in the department of Theatre, Film, and Dance (Jung, Film and Self-Knowledge), a graduate-level poetry workshop, and another undergraduate class in History of Art (Special Topics in Photography: American Memorial Portraits). Kierkegaard taught the last; he'd extended his stay in Ithaca. Frank was enrolled for credit and was the TA.

I considered telling him his scams made me feel stupid for following the rules and working hard, but I worried he'd simply tell me indeed I was stupid, there were too many loopholes to ignore, so instead I asked, "Are you going to grade your own papers in History of Art?"

He snorted lightly, unfazed by my sarcasm. "Come on, Han. I'm not writing papers."

22

The first party of the Fall semester was at Sam and Nat's. *Always a Bridesmaid,* the Xeroxed invitations read. Everyone had to wear bridesmaids' dresses—men and women—and I bought two of the ugliest Goodwill offered, mint green for me and metallic orange for Frank. On the way to the party he grumbled about how dumb the idea was, how the shiny fabric itched, how he was going to beat Todd's ass if he didn't show up in a dress. Frank hadn't shaved in a couple of days and I thought of Samuel Weed stumbling through the woods in an orange bridesmaid's dress about to be *betray'd by his Beard.*

"Lighten up," I told him. "You look cute."

He shook his head. "There'd better be a lot of beer."

Joanie was in antifreeze yellow with puff sleeves and black lace at the high neck and short hem. She wore a blue ribbon pinned to her chest; upon arrival she'd been awarded the grand prize; the judges felt there was no chance a more frightful entry would arrive.

When I congratulated her, Joanie shook her head and handed me a bottle of beer. "I had, no joke, a dozen fucking dresses to choose from."

"That's crazy! I had none. Always a bride, never a bridesmaid."

She looked me up and down. "Then where's that from?"

I was proud I'd found one so dreadful it fooled her. "Goodwill, nine bucks," I boasted. I fluffed my seafoam taffeta shirts.

Joanie and the six other women in the kitchen filed out silently, and for the next hour whenever I walked up to a conversation, it stopped. Even Todd, resplendent in a wedding gown, shunned me. With no one to talk to, I finished a beer quickly, then another. After a third, I found Frank alone in the bedroom petting Sam's huge cat, Panda.

"Let's go."

"Later," Frank told Panda, chucking him under the chin.

"I get the joke," he said bitterly while the Datsun warmed up, "but getting the joke doesn't make me feel normal wearing a dress."

"Why were the *lesbians* pissed at me?" The three beers made me tipsy and sad. "Sure, maybe Joanie's jealous, and maybe I shouldn't have joked about never being a bridesmaid, only a bride, but what the fuck?"

Frank braked for a red light. "I think Todd took a *picture* of me."

His selfish anger annoyed me. "*I'm* the one they won't talk to," I reminded him. "*I'm* the one they treat like shit because I got married. *I'm* the one who has to listen to lectures from professors about how disappointed they are by my heteronormativity." I kicked the glove compartment door and it fell open. "So don't complain to me about having spent the night petting a *cat*."

Frank pulled over and got out. A tiny old woman walking a tiny dog wearing a tiny sweater stopped under a streetlight. I watched her watch Frank tear off his orange dress. He split its seams, broke its zipper, wadded it into a ball, and threw it into the street. It looked like a smashed pumpkin. Underneath he wore only a jockstrap and running shoes. I saw the woman's lips silently form the words *Oh my,* and then Frank climbed back in and stomped on the gas. He was nearly naked and shivering—the Datsun's heater had gone out before I'd met him—and it was hard for me to stay angry as he shifted gears and responsibly signaled his turns while not wearing pants.

"Frank," I said gently, "is that a banana in your athletic supporter, or are you glad to see me?"

He looked down at his lap. "That's in repose, dear." He sounded tired. "Just wait and see what happens when I'm glad to see you."

23

I missed a period, waited two weeks to make sure it wasn't stress (Spenser presentation, Pound paper), found the left-over pregnancy test where I'd hidden it in the kitchen cabinet almost exactly a year before, and on the morning of October 13, 1991, peed on the stick while Frank snored. I matched the blue line to one pictured on the side of the box and quickly added dates. It had to have happened late in August. I went out into the cold apartment and shook Frank awake.

"They'll think they were right, but we were married." I held the stick in front of his face.

He squinted at it. "What *is* that?"

24

I wanted to try out the news before I called my mom, in part because Frank's excitement surprised me. I assumed he'd want to go to the drug store for another test, feared he'd want to talk about "options." Instead he kissed me and hugged me and called me "Little Momma." It was the first time being married made a difference. We lived in the same tiny apartment, I hadn't taken the time to get a new driver's license identifying me as Hannah Doyle, and a few months earlier pregnancy would've been trouble, but now it led to breakfast in bed and Frank boasting the pill couldn't stop him. I didn't have the heart to tell him I'd missed a few.

Frank's glee, so opposite what I'd expected, caused me to worry my mother's reaction would be equally contrary—not happy her married daughter would in nine months deliver a grandchild, but as if I were seventeen and Wes had knocked me up in the back of his Escort. I decided to rehearse the news on Pat Caldweel. I found her address in the phone book, wrapped up in the purple scarf, and left proud poppa to his pushups. Professor Caldweel lived in a shake-shingled cottage near the cemetery. She answered the door in sweatpants, a down vest, and a rainbow knit hat.

"Hannah? Is something wrong?"

I was grinning like an idiot. "Nope," I said, and shook my head to prove it.

"Come in, come in, come in," Professor Caldweel said, clearly puzzled.

"Nope," I repeated, then added a third, "Nope," hoping this would clear things up. We stood in a little living room painted white and filled with sleek, low black-leather-and-chrome furniture. It looked like a room in a design magazine.

I'd expected something different. I could see my breath. "It's cold in here."

"My furnace is out," she explained. "Come into the kitchen." The refrigerator had a glass door, rosemary grew in three identical glossy black pots on the windowsill, the countertops were white marble, gleaming copper pans hung on a rack over a huge stainless steel sink with a complicated spigot—another room out of *Architectural Digest*.

"Is something wrong?"

I rolled my tongue around my mouth, trying to find words to mimic the information I'd been able to share with Frank by showing him the blue line.

Pat Caldweel asked, "Tea?" just as I softly said, "Blue line."

"What?"

"I said, 'Yes, please.'"

She nodded and filled a little cup without a handle. "How's married life?" She made it sound like *lovely sky*.

I wanted her to be as excited and happy as Frank had been. "I'm pregnant!" I chirped.

Pat Caldweel took a long sip of her tea. "Well, that's great." Her voice was emotionless.

I imagined my mom using the same words and tone and my heart hurt.

"I've been worried about you," Professor Caldweel said, "because of Frank's troubles."

I was confused. "Frank's troubles?"

She sighed and I knew from the look on her face something bad was happening. "He hasn't told you?"

I imagined the lawyer father of an undergraduate girlfriend complaining to the dean. "Told me what?"

"He hasn't been attending classes, and there's talk of asking him to leave the program."

I was relieved—not an undergrad—then felt stupid for being relieved. He wasn't cheating on me, but he was in trouble for skipping class. I'd hoped for a cozy house filled with overstuffed chairs and books, my professor a stand-in for my mother, crying for joy at the news of my pregnancy, and instead I got a frigid magazine spread in which I was told my husband was about to be kicked out of graduate school for truancy.

"And Hannah? Some advice? Don't tell anyone about the baby until the second trimester. You never know."

I bit my lips to keep from crying or cussing.

My first impulse was to confront Frank and demand an explanation, but as I walked through the sharp October morning, it occurred to me Frank would answer by detailing systems that failed him and new ones he planned to employ. I'd hear about loopholes, contradictory catalogs, appeals, how professors in other departments loved to have grad students in their undergraduate classes. I kicked through a leaf pile in Dewitt Park, near the bench on which we'd sat one night in a long-ago July, and I decided I'd feign ignorance. If his systems worked, I didn't want to know how. If they didn't work, the outcome would be bad enough.

Then I wondered what he did instead of going to class. I tried to add up the running and the time in the gym and the time he admitted spending drinking coffee with the poets from the writing workshop he apparently wasn't going to, but even if he was all of those places when he claimed he was, hours and hours of each day were still left unaccounted for. I could pretend not to know he was skipping classes, but every cute co-ed I passed on my way home made me worry.

When I walked in, Frank was doing sit-ups on the kitchen linoleum, his toes under the stove. "Are you fucking your students? Sleeping with anyone but me?"

He looked baffled, then hurt. He solemnly crossed his heart and said, "No."

25

Ignorance of the systems Frank was using to keep from being dismissed from Cornell was good for me. If I'd known about them, the systems he invented in the name of helping me stay healthy while pregnant would've been unbearable. The day after I showed him the positive test, he informed me briefly what I should and should not eat, how much and what kind of exercise I should do, how much coffee I should drink (none), how much beer (none), how much wine (none). "I went to the library and read a book," he explained.

I watched him methodically scrub a mug I'd already washed and left to dry on the drainboard and in my head counted to three hundred to keep from telling him he should've gone to Jung, Film and Self-Knowledge instead of researching how many miles I should walk a week.

I suffered his regulations, attributing them to a combination of the same nervousness I felt about the baby, and to the ultimatums he'd apparently been given. He carefully graded student papers and wrote detailed, constructive commentaries. When he wasn't washing dishes or folding laundry, he was scribbling marginalia in his film studies textbook, in the ream-thick history of art course packet, and in the dainty collections of poems assigned as part of his creative writing class. One afternoon I walked past the dining hall on the way to the health center to buy neonatal vitamins and through a window saw him sitting at a table with Kierkegaard, dutifully taking notes while the professor talked and waved his hands. They were still there when I walked back, and I added an hour to Frank's timesheet, happy to find fewer and fewer moments for an affair.

He snatched a brown glass bottle of cream soda out of my hand one day, sipped it, looked guilty when it was not beer, but chided, "Sugar."

26

I turned twenty-four. Frank found time to knit me a yellow and green hat shaped like a huge buttercup flower with a six-inch stem and a leaf the size of my hand. He took me to dinner at Moosewood, ordered me dessert when I was in the bathroom, didn't blink when I ate it. Rarely did I suffer morning sickness, but I had to pee constantly, my jeans were quickly too tight to button, and I felt heavy and slow. I wore Frank's sweatpants and his puffy ski jacket and my upside-down flower hat. Classes were oddly easy, as if pregnancy made me smarter, somehow. Joanie and Nat and Sam were spread one each in my three seminars. I didn't speak to them, or they to me. I finished my papers early and turned them in weeks before they were due.

The days grew shorter and shorter and I felt lonely and fat and sometimes frightened by everything. One morning the sun didn't rise at all. I woke in the dark to see the numbers on the alarm clock flashing *3:13,* but I heard morning noises: the next-door neighbor's dog whining at the back door to be let in after yellowing the snow, kids at the bus stop hawking and spitting, the murmur of every radio in the building playing NPR—and then it occurred to me the clock's numbers recorded the hours and minutes that'd passed since the power had come on after failing, not the true time. Frank's hand was on my stomach, as if he'd been checking on the baby while he slept, maybe dreaming of it. What I'd mistaken for isolation I now recognized as the safety and comfort of true companionship. We didn't need other people. I let him sleep until there was barely enough time for him to dress and run to get to History of Art.

I roamed shops looking for the perfect Christmas gift for Frank. It needed to atone for the lack of gift the year before, and not remind him of his problems with school or of the impending change in his life that drew his hand to my belly while he slept. I found the dark green leather jacket in the window of a shop called Secondhand Cool that sold rare vinyl, used books, and consignment clothing. A snake biting its tail and twisted into an infinity symbol was embroidered across the shoulders in chartreuse thread.

"Rock star leather," the woman behind the counter said when I asked to see it. On her neck, below her left ear, was tattooed a tiny red-winged blackbird perched atop a teeny fencepost. The jacket was $350, a month's rent beyond the hundred-dollar budget I'd set for Frank's gift. I'd have to use my emergency VISA. "Aren't you Hannah?" They were in poetry workshop together. The coincidence earned me a fifty-dollar discount and a promise that Zöe wouldn't tell him about the gift.

Frank and I spent the break in Ithaca, and I pretended to ignore he was working frantically on papers he should've written during the semester and procrastinating almost equally frantically. I told myself he was freaked out by the pregnancy—I was, so it made some sense.

The night before Christmas we drank low-fat eggnog while watching a Rankin/Bass marathon on the little black-and-white: *Rudolph the Red-Nosed Reindeer, Santa Claus is Comin' to Town, Frosty the Snowman, A Year Without Santa Claus.* I retreated to bed to read while Frank watched the bizarre *Rudolph's Shiny New Year,* in which Rudolph teams up with a caveman, a medieval knight named Sir 1023, what looked like Ben Franklin, and Big Ben, a whale with a clock on his tail. Ten minutes into *Jack Frost*, a droll folktale narrated by a groundhog named Pardon-me-Pete with Buddy Hackett's voice, I grew desperate and demanded, "Turn that off and come fuck me." He obeyed.

On Christmas morning we sat Indian-style before the two-foot pine bough Frank snapped off a campus tree and I decorated with drug store tinsel. We took turns tearing wrapping paper, Frank first.

He whispered, "Where did you find this?" as if I'd given him a passenger pigeon in a parakeet cage. He put the jacket on over the long underwear he'd worn to bed. It was a perfect fit. In his thermal shirt and the jacket, he looked like a rock star. "Now you."

The first package held the little book I'd abandoned in Professor Presley's hands. I was dumbfounded. I never told Frank how hurt I'd been by Presley's hypocrisy, never told him Presley's dismissal of the little book had caused me to question if what I did at Cornell held any value. "How?" I asked.

"The janitors like me. Open the other one."

It was a tiny red sweater and a bright red hat shaped like a tomato top, with a green stem and two knitted leaves.

"I've been too busy," he apologized, and I could tell from his face he was about to confess why he'd been so busy.

Before he could, I said, "Make me some hot chocolate?"

27

On December 31, after working on a paper all morning, Frank claimed a craving for circus peanuts and strapped on his snowshoes. It took me fifteen minutes to work up the courage to call my mother. When I told her I was pregnant, she cried happily.

"So that's why you two didn't come for Christmas! You didn't want to travel in your condition!"

"That's it, that's it." I was pleased to be gifted the excuse. "And I didn't want to tell you before the first trimester was over."

28

Beer, which I wasn't allowed even to sip, had to go from grocery bag to freezer for one hour of chilling—even though the trip from store to home was through January's chill—and then into the *back* of the fridge. Breakfast was oatmeal sweetened with honey, decaffeinated Earl Grey lightened with low-fat milk, and a banana. Frank made me the same sack lunch every day: peanut butter and sliced apples on wheat, two yogurts (one blueberry, one strawberry), and three bananas. Dinner was vegetables and tofu, prepared in ways he claimed made each night's meal different, but didn't. Bedtime snack was a banana and sixteen ounces of 2%.

I smiled when he chided me for wasting dental floss—"You don't need two feet"—and bit my tongue while he demonstrated how to make do with six inches. The new semester was hard on him, I knew. He was enrolled in seminars on Milton, Henry and William James, and Shakespeare's romances. Instead of teaching or TAing, he tutored football and basketball players and worked as a research assistant for an emeritus professor who'd been writing a biography of William Dean Howells for twenty-five years. Frank made it sound as if these were his choices, but during a meeting I scheduled with her to discuss a directed reading project on Puritan sermons, Pat Caldweel confided Frank had been told what classes to take, that the English department had farmed him out to athletics, and his duties as assistant to Professor Krehbiel included fetching coffee and library books and helping the old man across icy sidewalks to and from his car.

"He's lucky. A few years ago a grad student in physics sued when her support was revoked after her students complained all she did in labs was lecture them on how racist and homophobic they were. She lost, but it was ugly. If it wasn't for her, Frank would be out on his ass."

Another loophole, I thought, and he didn't even know about this one—I hoped.

Professor Caldweel covered her sad, stern face with her hands, and when she uncovered it, she smiled and beamed at me. Her peek-a-boo transformation freaked me out.

"So how're you feeling?"

"Fine," I mumbled. "Always hungry." I kept to myself I was always horny.

After the meeting, on my way to an appointment for a twenty-week ultrasound, I craved forbidden sugar and sinful salt. I told myself if Frank could keep from me why he was taking specific classes, I could keep from him what I ate when he wasn't around, and I stopped at a convenience store and bought a bottle of Gatorade, a box of frosted strawberry PopTarts, and a family-size bag of Cool Ranch Doritos. The parking lot was paved in dirty snow. The apartment was a dozen cold blocks away.

"Can I stand here?" I asked the dreadlocked white teenager behind the counter. I pointed to the scuffed floor in front of the magazine rack. The kid shrugged. I turned my back to him and methodically began to eat six jam-sweet PopTarts, then the salad dressing-flavored corn chips. When I chugged the bottle of lemon-lime Gatorade—sweet and salty—I felt the baby wiggle for the first time. I put my hand on my belly and saw the kid staring at me in the convex security mirror.

"I'm pregnant," I told his funhouse reflection, "not high. Were I high, I'd be drinking malt liquor, not Gatorade, okay?"

He touched two fingers to his temple in halfhearted salute. "It's all good."

Frank was supposed to meet me at the doctor's office, but he didn't show up before the nurse called my name. The ultrasound room was cluttered with equipment and dimly lit; there were more chairs than were necessary; it felt like a supply closet, not part of a medical facility. The technician was a grinning woman with a round face and dreadlocks who wore tie-dyed pants under her lab coat. She looked like she could be the convenience store kid's mom.

I listened to the *whoosh-whoosh-whoosh* of the baby's heartbeat and tried to make out shapes in the mess on the little screen. "There." The technician pointed, and I saw a baby. I watched the grainy ghost thrashing in darkness.

"That's one active kid," the technician said. "You drink some juice before you came in?"

"Organic apple," I lied.

The technician moved the ultrasound thingy across my belly and I was sure I saw a tiny profile with my nose. The woman moved it again and cocked her head. "This is pretty early, but that juice is making this one immodest, and it looks like"—the baby kicked, the technician clicked a button, and the image on the screen froze—"it's a girl." The woman tapped the picture. "Those are labia."

For the first time I had to admit I'd been hoping for a daughter, dreading a son. "Thank God," I said.

The technician laughed.

Frank wasn't in the waiting room. I hurried home, hoping he'd gone there when he'd realized he'd forgotten the appointment. The apartment was empty, and there was no note, but my rewashed breakfast dishes were still wet. I fought the urge to call my mother. The news was too good to keep to myself but too special to share with anyone else but Frank first. A few months before, I would've had no idea where to look for him, but now I knew he'd gone to campus. I found the Datsun's extra key in the magnetic box stuck under the bumper—the January air was cold enough to burn my face and getting colder, so there was no way I was going to walk, plus in my condition a fall on an icy sidewalk could lead to more than just a sore ass, plus I knew Frank's route and might be able to catch up in the car. The radio was tuned to the Ithaca College student station and "Smells Like Teen Spirit" was playing, as it almost always was. I turned it up and hummed along while the car stuttered itself warm.

I didn't see his green leather jacket anywhere along the way. I parked as close to the library as I could and went to check my carrel. I'd given Frank the key when I found out he'd lost his office along with his teaching appointment, and when the apartment grew too small, that's where he went to study. He didn't answer when I knocked, and I didn't hear anything when I put my ear to the thin door.

"Hannah?" a woman's voice whispered, and I jumped. Joanie poked her head from her carrel, two down from mine.

"Seen Frank?" I whispered back, the first words I'd spoken to her in more than a month.

She shook her head. "I've been here for a few hours, and I haven't heard him. He's hardly ever here."

"You were wrong. I wasn't pregnant before I got married."

Joanie nodded. "I guessed as much."

"*Shut it*," a voice from another carrel snapped.

Joanie rolled her eyes with great exaggeration. "Steve, my new sexy boyfriend. Sociology. I'd introduce you, but he's way, way too hot. It'd be like watching cows fucking, or whatever's supposed to mess up unborn babies."

"Talking in a library?" unseen Steve suggested.

I hadn't known how lonely I was until I had to fight the urge to hug Joanie and tell her the baby was a girl. "I have to find Frank," I whispered.

There was no sign of him when I got home. The answering machine blinked. I expected to hear Frank's voice apologizing; instead, a female version of that voice identified itself as his cousin Alice and told him his aunt—also named Alice—was dead. He had never mentioned either Alice, and I felt foolish for assuming orphan Frank was completely alone, no living cousins, aunts, et cetera.

I heard him stomping snow off his boots on the porch while I wrote down the information his cousin offered about the funeral arrangements. "I hope you and Hannah can come, since you're my only family now," Alice said. She knew my name.

When he opened the door, I told him, "You missed the ultrasound appointment."

"*Damn it,*" he barked, as if he'd stubbed his toe. "I'm sorry, Han. I forgot it was today. Is everything okay?"

I nodded.

He hugged me and I spoke into the shoulder of his green jacket. "Swear you'll do one thing for me, and I'll tell you if it's a boy or a girl."

He tightened his hug. "Okay, tell me."

"One thing."

"Okay, deal—tell me."

"It's a girl."

"All right!" he cheered.

I hugged him back, happy he was happy. I felt guilty for thinking I'd have to trick him to get him to go to his aunt's funeral. "Your cousin called. I'm sorry—your aunt died. Alice wants us to come to the funeral."

He let go of me. "We're not going," he said flatly, and I no longer felt guilty.

"We made a deal." I pushed the answering machine's play button and watched Frank listen to the message. I was ready to tell him I knew he'd been demoted to football tutor, knew he was rarely in my library carrel. I was ready to remind him I wasn't the one who'd fucked up, I was the one who kept appointments, I was the one who told him about my cousins in Spokane.

Frank sighed when the message ended, pushed play again and slapped his pockets, feeling for a pen.

"I wrote it all down," I told him.

"Thanks," he said. "A daughter." He reached out and touched my belly. "A *daughter*."

29

I hadn't calculated how miserable I'd be—five months pregnant, wrapped in a blanket in the unheated Datsun, in late January, in Upstate New York and northern Ohio, headed for a funeral in a city cringing on the edge of Lake Erie. I needed to pee constantly, but forced myself to wait until I could barely hold it before begging Frank to take the next exit. We wore scarves over our mouths to keep the windshield clear since the defroster was dead. I felt guilty for feeling uncomfortable when I considered how he was surely suffering—I hadn't thought about his parents and his brother when I forced him to keep his side of the bargain.

I tried to joke about the adventure, but when all I got out of Frank were muffled grunts, I gave up and read a book about Native Americans who'd traveled with Buffalo Bill's Wild West show. It'd been shelved beside the monograph I'd meant to get, one about earlier Indians who'd been displayed in European capitals, but after I mistakenly checked it out, I decided to read it for fun over the break.

In Erie, Pennsylvania we stopped at a Denny's for coffee and soup.

"When the Wild West went to Rome, the Pope blessed the Indians," I shared with Frank.

"Huh," he said, then slurped his beef-vegetable.

"Ah, yes, the spirited back-and-forth of intellectual discourse."

"Han, I've got frostbite on my ass because you want to go to the funeral of someone you never met and I barely knew, so don't hassle me, okay?"

"I'm cold too."

"Wouldn't be if you'd listened to me."

"Hey," I chirped, "I have an idea, why don't you slap your pregnant wife to keep her in her place?"

"Hannah, don't be a bitch."

I was dumbstruck—for a moment—and then I flipped his soup bowl into his lap and got up from the booth. The bathroom was as icy as the car. I pulled down my pants and sat on the freezing toilet and shivered angrily. I wanted him to say something about his parents, to tell me he was sad. Frank was gone when I came back to the table. Neat piles of coins held down a ten-dollar bill.

"He's getting gas," the waitress told me. She looked to be in her sixties at least. On her nametag, *Paula* was handwritten above *Trainee*. "He said he didn't want you to have to wait in the cold."

I considered telling Paula I had a good reason for dumping soup on thoughtful Frank's crotch, but instead I nodded and looked out at the pumps next door. There was no sign of the Datsun and for a moment I thought he'd ditched me, then I saw him sitting in the car where he'd parked, forehead against the steering wheel.

Paula had jumper cables in her truck, but the Datsun wouldn't even crank, let alone start. I sat behind the wheel turning the key while Frank ducked under the hood and the sexagenarian trainee waitress gunned her pickup's engine. As soon as we gave up, a tow truck pulled into the parking lot. The driver was a teenager in a bright orange snowsuit that made him look like a little boy. He greeted Paula by name and then kindly asked Frank, "Piss yourself?" pointing to the dark spot now flecked with stars of frost.

Frank shook his head. "Soup."

Even the tow truck's more powerful jump could not revive the little car. "How much will you give me for the tires?" Frank asked.

The kid bent and examined the tread. "You put these on this morning?"

"Almost," Frank said.

I had no idea the tires were new—and when the kid offered a hundred dollars, I wondered if he was being kind or taking advantage. How much did tires cost?

"And you take us to the bus," Frank bargained.

He surprised me when he bought one-way tickets to Cleveland. I'd assumed we'd head back to Ithaca, not continue on to the funeral. The bus was warm, there were two seats together, the lavatory was only a few paces away. Frank went to sleep, or pretended to, and I read my book and listened to the murmur of several conversations until I dozed.

Frank nudged me awake. "Behold my homeland." He rapped the smeared window. Cleveland from the highway looked like Richmond, Atlanta, Knoxville. I searched for something to comment upon and found nothing. I watched him staring at the generic skyline and wondered if he was thinking about Harmon, his dad, his mom.

"What're you thinking?"

He shook his head. "Stupid."

"Excuse me?"

"Not you, me. I was thinking about something stupid. Girl I went to a basketball game with in high school."

I felt like I was reading his diary. "And?" I asked, hoping he'd turn the page.

He smirked at Cleveland. "I took this girl named Stephanie to an away game—she asked me to take her. My junior year. We lost. Our basketball team sucked. We got Burger King afterward, and then on the way to her house she kept pointing out playgrounds, church parking lots, the elementary school we both went to. I thought she might be nervous about her curfew or something, so I ran yellow lights and hurried, but then I couldn't figure out why she was so pissed when I got her home. I was a few blocks away, sitting at a stop sign beside one of the playgrounds she'd pointed out, when it hit me she'd been suggesting places to park." He shook his head. "See? Stupid."

"I think it's sweet."

Frank shrugged. "She *was* cute."

The bus left the highway and descended onto surface streets. The windows of the storefronts not covered with yellowed newspaper or plywood were filled with hand-lettered placards rife with misspellings and odd capitalizations. The dingy Greyhound station looked spiffy in comparison. Gritty wind stung my face when I stepped off the bus.

"I need to call Alice," Frank said. "I hope I can catch her."

There was a Denny's across the street. I pointed. "Call her from there. I'm hungry."

"Again?"

"Pregnant, remember?" I rubbed my belly with both hands and then checked my watch. "And I ate *soup* two hours ago."

I sipped decaf and watched Frank at the payphone. I hoped he'd tell me another anecdote like the one about Stephanie who'd wanted to make out, and such an anecdote would lead to something about his family. He nodded at the wall and hung up.

"Do you keep the car running?" I asked when he sat down.

"What?"

"When you make out in Cleveland in a car in winter."

He shrugged. "I'm the wrong person to ask." He studied the laminated menu as if it might hold different choices than it had in Erie. "Alice is going to pick us up. She might know." He flipped the menu from burgers to breakfasts.

"I'm getting a patty melt with fries and a chocolate shake." The meal was intended to annoy him—greasy, sweet, fried. I'd pick a fight if it took that to get him talking.

He nodded. "I think I'll have an omelet."

I gave up and asked, "Are you upset about your mom and dad and Harmon?"

Frank started. "What?"

"Are you upset about your mom and dad and Harmon?"

He shrugged. "Always."

I took a deep breath and watched him run his finger under the list of side items. Clearly he was playing dumb, and I knew I should drop it, but sitting in a Denny's in Cleveland, pregnant with his baby, I wanted my husband to tell me something—*anything*—about how he felt to be back in the town in which he'd buried his entire family. "Did the crash happen in the winter?"

"Hannah, I love you, but I don't want to talk about it."

"I feel like there are too many things you don't want to talk about—and please don't shrug your shoulders."

He rubbed his temples and spoke into his palms. "It happened in June. My dad ran a red light and a truck hit them. It was a beer delivery truck, Budweiser. I made a deal with the hospital to take all the organs they could use in exchange for free cremation. I scattered some of my mom's ashes in the Botanical Garden, some of Harmon's down by the lake where he and his skater friends smoked dope and got drunk, some in the parking lot behind the Methodist church where he and his basketball friends smoked dope and got drunk. I had to sneak my dad's into Municipal Stadium in a Zip-Loc bag during an Indians game, and I got thrown out when an usher saw me drop a handful onto the field."

The waiter came to the table and licked his pen and Frank calmly ordered. "She'll have a patty melt with fries and a large chocolate shake and I'll have a garden omelet with hash browns, please."

"Right up," the waiter said.

Frank looked at me and started to shrug, caught himself, and froze with his shoulders lifted. "Sorry."

"It's okay. Finish your shrug." A cold breeze wrapped around my ankles and I looked over his falling shoulder at the door. A woman who looked like Frank scanned the room. "Alice," I said, and waved.

Frank turned in his seat and Alice mirrored Frank's grin—lopsided, dimpled, squinting. They could've been twins. I realized I was staring and Alice had been holding out her hand for several seconds. I took it and shook.

"I guess he didn't mention we kind of look alike?"

"Kind of?"

Alice laughed and slid into the booth beside me. "Stop me when I tell you something you know, okay? My mother was Frank's father's sister, and my father his mother's brother. His parents met at my parents' wedding—they were best man and maid of honor—and they eloped the next day."

I was astonished. Not mentioning a cousin and an aunt in Cleveland could be explained—I hadn't yet laid out a detailed family tree for Frank—but not sharing a story like that was keeping a secret.

"My mother never forgave her brother and her sister-in-law," Alice said. "She always felt they'd made her wedding shabby. Frank and I were, what, nine? ten? *eleven?* before we met, and we lived maybe five miles from each other."

Frank got up. "I need to use the bathroom."

As he walked away, the waiter arrived. I saw Alice frown at my burger and the cherry atop the whipped cream capping my huge milkshake. "I'm five months pregnant," I explained, and then worried that was exactly why she was frowning.

Alice chuckled and shook her head. "Hannah, he doesn't tell anybody anything. I figured you were fat."

It felt better than it should've to know I was not alone in the dark.

"Quick, while he's gone, tell me everything. Girl or boy? What're you studying? What's he studying?"

"It's a girl," I said, and Alice high-fived me. I told her about women's Indian captivity narratives and how I was thinking of comparing them to the narratives of Indians who'd traveled to Europe around the same time. My heart sank when I tried to explain Frank's studies. What was he studying? "He's interested in film," I lamely offered, and Alice nodded.

"We have a Native American great-great-grandmother. Her name was Susan—how's that for exotic? Our grandfather—Frank's dad's father, my mom's dad—changed her tribe each time he told me about her. Sometimes she was Seneca, sometimes Navajo, once Flathead. I always hoped Flathead was right."

I divided in my head. "That makes your generation one-sixteenth?"

"That sounds about right." She took a French fry off my plate. "Don't you think we all must have about a sixteenth of everything in us by now?"

I imagined the cemetery was beautiful in summertime, but in January the trees were skeletal and the dead grass was scabbed with patches of dirty snow. The backhoe that'd broken the frozen earth was parked a few hundred yards away under a black tarpaulin that rattled in the wind. When he arrived, the priest was wearing an orange and yellow-striped balaclava above his cleric's collar. He shook my hand with a huge puffy mitten. He took off the ski mask to read a quick eulogy, but kept his mittens on.

Alice and Frank's matching frowns tightened when the painful wind blew in their faces. I was happy I'd made Frank come to the funeral, happy I'd pried a few facts and feelings from him and gotten from Alice some information about his family. The cold came up through the soles of my shoes, between buttons and snaps. I thought I felt the baby flinch when an especially icy wind blasted the graveyard. What bothered me was the feeling each tidbit Frank let me taste was evidence he was hiding a storehouse of goodies.

The young priest said, "Amen," and we echoed him. The cousins walked a few steps toward the backhoe and bent toward each other, foggy breathes mixing between their faces. I watched the priest watching them, clearly taken aback by the likeness. He saw me watching and smiled. Frank hugged Alice and then shook the priest's hand.

"She gave us the car." He showed me the key. "It was Aunt Alice's."

Gratitude rendered me speechless. I hugged Alice.

The red Honda Civic turned over smoothly and its heater pumped warm air almost immediately. "Wait," I said. "How's she going to get home?"

"They're dating."

Alice and the priest were getting into his Jeep.

"You look shocked. He's not Catholic."

"I thought he was gay."

Frank signaled for a left turn at the cemetery's gate. "Not in Cleveland."

30

I read the *Chronicle of Higher Education* in bed, wearing my buttercup hat and a pair of gloves. After Cleveland, I'd had trouble feeling warm. Only when I was under two quilts or in the Honda with the heater cranked up all the way and blowing hotly in my face did the chill leave my bones. Across the small room Frank sat in a T-shirt and sweatpants, his bare feet on the sill of the drafty window, reading an Erskine Caldwell novel I'd been assigned in a Southern literature class while an undergrad at Tennessee.

"Hey, listen to this: *The University of Nebraska-Lincoln invites applications from scholars of Native American descent for a two-year post-doctoral Native American Studies research and teaching fellowship.* Too bad you don't know which tribe your great-great-granny Susan was from and too bad you're not post-doc and too bad you don't do Native American Studies." I tapped the next page. "You think I could convince Cal State-Fresno I'm a specialist in Irish theatrical literature and culture of the late Nineteenth Century?" I was reading the *Chronicle* in preparation for a meeting that afternoon, and I was amazed by the announcements of esoteric fellowships, narrowly-defined jobs, and calls for papers I thought might be jokes. "Want to write an essay about *Star Trek* and Lacan?"

A professor named Jenks led the once-a-semester professional development seminar. He was in his mid-fifties but youthful behind his gray beard. His uniform was hiking boots, jeans, a pressed shirt, a tweed jacket with elbow patches, and a tie with orange and blue stripes I assumed signaled he'd attended a New England prep school and/or Princeton. I was surprised and relieved to find Joanie and Zöe the poet outside the room. Jenks's clinics on how to get ahead in academia were mocked as being only for desperate tools. I'd signed up because when my mother asked the week before, I couldn't explain exactly how one got a job as an English professor.

"Jenks's meeting?"

Zöe nodded. "But you're skipping. Baby shower."

"Baby shower?"

"Surprise!" Joanie sang.

Professor Jenks turned the corner shuffling note cards and Zöe put her hand on my forehead. "You do feel hot."

"Hannah might have a fever—and she's pregnant," Joanie told him.

He nodded seriously. "I'll leave handouts in your boxes."

"That would be rad," Zöe said, and I coughed to cover my laugh.

"Get her some broth," Jenks suggested.

"Yes, broth," Joanie agreed.

At Nat and Sam's house pink bunting and ribbons hung from the living room ceiling and there were gifts on the coffee table. A cake decorated with a marzipan pacifier and rattle had *It's A Girl!* written on it in pink icing. I was so touched I thought I might cry. "Who told you it's a girl?"

"Frank," Joanie said. "She's all he talks about."

"You sisters sure know how to go femme when the situation demands," Zöe said to Nat.

Sam appeared in the kitchen door with a bottle of red in one hand and a bottle of white in the other. "Let's get shitfaced while she opens presents stone sober," she cheerily suggested. "Some tap water, Hannah?"

"She's kidding," Joanie said. "About the tap water, at least. I got Gatorade for you—Frank says you like lemon-lime best."

Inside the boxes there were bibs and baby bottles, blankets and booties. I ate cake and happily listened to Nat and Sam and Joanie and Zöe joke about diapers and turkey basters. Friendship amazed me. A few weeks ago I was sure none of these women would ever speak to me again and I was convinced I never wanted to speak to them, and now they were drinking Gatorade between glasses of wine and teasing me about birth control.

"I wish my mom were here," I told them.

Nat laughed. "Either you're suffering some hormonal weirdness, or your mom's a lot cooler than mine, or both."

"Okay," Joanie said, "I've got to know. Is the screwing better, worse, or just different?"

I felt my face go hot. "I want it all the time," I admitted, and everyone laughed. "But I worry Frank doesn't."

"That poem, though," Zöe said.

I was confused. "What poem?"

"The one about you two doing it now that you're pregnant."

"He wrote a *poem* about that?" I felt an amplified version of the embarrassment I suffered each time Kierkegaard greeted me in the library. "And turned it in to *class?*"

"All his poems are about you," Zöe said. "But they're not all about doing it. He's never shown you his poems?"

"He told me they were no good."

Zöe made a face. "He lies. They're great. I hate him because they're so good and he doesn't care. I'm too buzzed to remember exactly, but the one about you being pregnant is all about how cool it is to have hot sex with the same woman every night who is not the same woman every night."

"Poor Hannah," Joanie moaned in fake sorrow. "Married to a cruel, cruel man who writes poems about how he's got a constant boner for her while she's with child."

Nat was at the window, surveying the white lawn with a serious look on her face. "Let's go outside and make snow individuals," she suggested.

I had to call Frank for a ride, so drunk were my friends. They were chewing on bubblegum cigars when he came to the door. There was much winking and elbowing as he bent over to gather up baby loot.

In the car he asked, "Want to do something kinky?"

"Please," I said, hoping and worrying we were on our way to a parking lot as the sun dimmed. Kinky was good, but cold would be a problem. I turned up the heater. I wanted him to recite the poem, wanted to thank him for boasting about the baby and for knowing which flavor of Gatorade I preferred.

The apartment was toasty as the car, banging radiator fogging the windows. The little black and white showed a shot of the empty bed. The toy camera was balanced between two stacks of books on a chair, humming mechanically. I worried.

"It's not recording," he said, reading my mind. "It's on pause. So we can watch."

Frank had placed the camera so we appeared to be blissfully gazing off into glowing space when we looked at ourselves. On TV, my pale belly was the moon.

31

Pregnancy made February in Ithaca twice as depressing. I couldn't escape the chill that snuck under the door, up through the ugly carpet squares stuck to the floor, the chill that kept the tub icy no matter how hot I ran the water. Six months along, I figured the extra weight I was carrying should heat me up, but it didn't.

My upstairs neighbor, a round Ukrainian with a hairdo and beard like Grizzly Adams, with whom I'd exchanged maybe three words in a year and a half, left a typed note informing me he was moving to Boca Raton at the end of May, and he and the landlord had discussed the fact his apartment was more suitable for a couple with a newborn than the studio I now occupied, so on June 1, 1992, I and Frank and the baby would move into the two-bedroom he was vacating, and my rent would increase by sixty-five dollars. The note annoyed me. It read like an eviction notice more than a kind offer. We *would* move in June, not we *could*. I showed it to Frank and was surprised when he said only, "That's good news."

His classes seemed to be going well, and his systems had dwindled to dishwashing and bed-making. Hiding from the cold in the apartment, the hectic first month of the semester over, I sorted library books to take back before the baby was born. At the bottom of a stack I found the monograph about Buffalo Bill's Wild West and opened it to the dog-eared page where I'd stopped reading on the way back from Cleveland. Pat Caldweel had scowled and advised, "Don't lose focus" when I mentioned enjoying the book.

I flipped through the last chapters and my eye fell on a sentence inside parentheses: *(Because he feared for their safety while imprisoned, Cody used his influence to effect the release into his custody a number of survivors of the Wounded Knee Massacre. These Lakota Sioux performed as part of the Wild West during the show's European tour of 1891–1892.)*

There was no tiny superscript number leading to an endnote, no further mention of the survivors in the index. My hands shook. I put on my coat and my scarf and then took them off. The index was nearly as long as the book itself. The reference had to be obscure, maybe even untrustworthy, but that didn't matter.

I composed my essay over the next two weeks, calmly sitting in my library carrel from eight in the morning to noon, penciling each day seven hundred and fifty words onto the pages of a yellow legal pad. I felt no need to rush to record my ideas. For months I'd fed information into the little machine inside my head—the two versions of Sarah Weed's narrative of captivation by Indians, one in which her husband cowered in a dress, the other in which he died bravely defending her; Pocahontas watching a Ben Johnson masque in London with King James; Buffalo Bill saving Ghost Dancers from prison by having them play Indians in a show about the Wild West that toured Europe; Michel Foucault's *Discipline and Punish*. The little machine sorted and cross-referenced and connected. For months I'd been writing the essay while I slept, worried about Frank, worried about giving birth, worried about taking care of the baby, had sex. All I had to do was transcribe, and while the calm I felt was almost disappointing, I couldn't deny the thirty pages were perfect—too perfect to share. I couldn't take the chance that instead of praising my work Pat Caldweel might scold me for losing focus. On the last day of February I typed up and printed the essay, deleted the file from my Mac's hard drive, put the printout in an unlabeled manila folder, and slid the folder between one holding my soon-to-be-obsolete lease and one holding a copy of my 1990 1040EZ.

32

I began to have trouble keeping track of the calendar. The expiration date on the milk jug confounded me. Was it still potable if scheduled to sour on March 11? I developed a crush on the nurse who called the day before to remind me of appointments with the OB-GYN. I stuck a piece of tape with the number for time and temperature on the base of the phone and developed a second crush on the robotic baritone I listened to while checking syllabi or fretting over the bowl of breakfast cereal that tasted a little off.

I asked my mother to call each Wednesday at noon. I told her that was a time and day I was sure to be free and at home, and while it was true, I also wanted a way to mark the center of the week. When one Friday morning Mom called, I thought it was midday Wednesday and freaked out. I hadn't even looked at the cover of the book I was supposed to have read for my Thursday seminar, a seminar I was sure I'd just sat through the day before. I studied the wall calendar hanging beside the fridge.

"What's today's date?" I whined.

"Friday the ninth," my mother said. "Do you know where I stored those Easter bonnets?"

"It's already Easter? How did I miss Spring Break?"

"Jesus, Hannah, calm down and listen to me, *It's the ninth of March.* Isn't your break the week after next?"

I took a deep breath and read *SPRING BREAK!* inked in green across the week of March 19. "Yes." I flipped to April. "And Easter is the fifteenth of next month."

"Are you all right?" She sounded worried. "Is Frank there?"

"I'm fine. The bonnets are in the guestroom closet, up above my prom dress."

"Is Frank there?"

I had no idea where Frank was, when he'd left, if he'd told me where he was going or when he'd be back. "He just went out to get me some circus peanuts."

Mom laughed. "I wanted garlic bread and candy bars all the time when I was pregnant with you."

I wrote *today* in the square for Friday, March 9, and said, "I have to go."

"Give my love to Frank."

"Will do." My breath smelled sour. I hung up, blew into a cupped hand, sniffed.

My toothbrush was dry and I couldn't remember if I'd used it earlier. I bared my teeth and looked into the mirror. I flossed and brushed and gargled with Frank's nasty yellow Listerine and still felt filthy. The towel over the bar was damp, but Frank could've used it after his shower, so there was no telling when I'd last bathed. I stuck my nose into an armpit and below the Teen Sprit deodorant I'd chosen as a joke, I smelled what could've been days of sweat.

In the shower I soaped myself with Frank's bar of Irish Spring until my eyes burned and lathered my hair with Herbal Essence over and over until I lost count of rinses and repeats. Worries led to other worries, and I feared every choice I'd made was a mistake. I wasn't cut out for motherhood, for marriage, for graduate school. What had I been thinking? I eased down into the tub and while I shaved my legs—at least a week's growth, if not more—I decided to give up the child for adoption, divorce Frank, and drop out of school. My belly was huge. What kind of pervert found that attractive? What was *wrong* with him? I closed the taps with my feet and sat with my eyes shut listening to the last of the water gurgling down the drain.

I wiped the fogged mirror with a washcloth and took a good look at myself. The PixelVision camera's soft focus and the TV's small screen had shown a different woman than the one I now saw. This one looked tired. At last I had the boobs I'd wanted at age fourteen, though, a thought that made me smile. My belly button had flipped from innie to outie. No wonder I couldn't keep track of time, no wonder books couldn't hold my attention, no wonder I worried I was too scatterbrained to remember to brush my teeth, let alone to be able to take care of a baby—in two months that baby would be in my arms, not inside me. I wasn't unable to focus; I was, in fact, so focused that time, books, classes, and brushing my teeth had become unimportant, even though I tried to distract myself by worrying about them. One look in the mirror and I knew nature had won. From now on, the baby owned my every thought. The little machine offered up one last word—*Ava*—and turned itself off.

33

My address was early on the mailman's route. Some days it was just after I drank my second or third decaf that between houses I espied him delivering the next block's mail. His appearance signaled the end of lazy morning. When I saw him, I called the time and temperature, took a shower, dressed, fetched the bills and coupons and envelops of pictures of me as a baby my mother had begun to send, and then depending on the day of the week either caught the shuttle to campus, or sat in bed and tried to keep warm while I read.

The cherries were blooming in Nashville, my mother bragged. In Ithaca the third week of March lifted the sky's gray lid and let in a little light. A threadbare robin joined the winter birds at the feeder. Soon tulips would groan in their beds and the gothic trees would bud.

Six mailboxes hung in a row beside what was once a farmhouse's front door. The house had been split into apartments and Farm Street's name was all that remained of the farm. My box was last in line. A rolled manila envelope was jammed into it, and I worried Mom had sent 8×10s now surely bent and creased. When I pulled it from the box, I recognized Frank's handwriting. The envelope was addressed to a scholarly journal at Eastern Washington University and had been returned because of insufficient postage. It was a relief to find Frank was submitting articles, but I felt a little guilty he was sending them on the sly—I worried he felt the need to hide even potential failures.

Our unspoken agreement not to discuss his problems at school limited conversation, and because I didn't want to bug him or seem trivial, I kept to myself a lot of what I thought about the baby. I hadn't told him I'd decided our little girl's name would be Ava. Zöe had to tell me about the poetry Frank wrote. I pulled the rest of the mail from the box and vowed to be less critical so he would be more forthcoming with his emotions and thoughts and poems. Even if I didn't say anything, surely he could tell I was disappointed he'd nearly been expelled.

There was also a business-sized envelope for Frank with a University of Nebraska return address. The baby kicked and I remembered I hadn't yet eaten breakfast.

I fixed a bowl of instant oatmeal and opened a bottle of Gatorade and examined the returned envelope. I decided it would be best to put it back in the box and ask Frank to check the mail when he got home. He hadn't licked the glue on the flap, and only the metal clasp held the envelope closed. I'd read hardly anything he'd written. Daily I resisted the urge to open his files on the Mac because I worried his rushed work wouldn't warrant the A-minus he always managed, or it would be better than the work I dutifully labored over for weeks. If he felt this was good enough to send out—or if a professor told him it was that good—I wanted to see it, at least to find out what it was about. Silence? Jung? The James brothers? I could peek before I put it back in the mailbox and he'd never know.

Beneath a letter asking the editors to find enclosed his article, which Frank wished to submit for their review and for possible publication, was the essay I'd written and hidden and told no one about.

I opened the envelope from Nebraska, hoping whatever was inside might explain what was happening, and it did. A congratulatory note on UN-L letterhead informed Frank he'd been awarded the two-year post-doctoral teaching and research fellowship for Native Americans for which he'd applied—and in so doing informed me my husband had progressed from loophole-exploiter to flat-out liar.

The baby kicked hard, and when I pressed my hand to my belly, I felt through my shirt the imprint of Ava's tiny foot. I wanted to cry. I felt stupid for not leaving Frank when I had the chance, before I was married and pregnant and before I loved him as much as I did. I tried to calm down by remembering why I loved him: his grin, the way he knew to back me up when I needed support and tell me I was full of shit when I was full of shit, twisting Todd's arm until he apologized, the poems Zöe told me about, the silent movie he'd made of me asleep, the scarf he'd knit, the way he folded my clothes and cooked for me.

No one had seen the essay. Frank wasn't Native American and wouldn't have a Ph.D. by August, two requirements the letter reminded him he'd need to fulfill. In a way all this trouble was moot. I wanted apologies, however. I'd forgotten what day it was already, so I dialed time and temperature. Tuesday—he'd be home for lunch soon.

I filled the teakettle with milk, lit the eye under it, and spun the knob until the burner roared. I sat down at the table and waited.

Boiling milk was bubbling from the spout and scorching on the side of the kettle when he opened the door. "What the hell?" he yelped, rushing to wrap his hand in a dishtowel and lift the stinking, smoking thing from the stovetop. He set it in the sink and it hissed when he ran water over it. "You ruined this."

"It's mine," I told him, surprised by how calm I was managing to be.

"It's ruined."

"It's mine," I repeated, this time not so calmly. "And so is this table and so are these chairs and so is that futon and so is the computer and so are the forks and knives and spoons and so are the washrags and the bookshelves and the books and the lamps and the measuring cups and the *motherfucking cookie sheets.*"

"What're you talking about?"

"Nothing is yours, Frank. I was thinking about it, and it occurred to me *nothing* in this apartment is yours."

"Is this some kind of pregnancy thing?"

"No, *Frank*, this is some kind of nothing-is-yours thing." I stood up and threw the manila envelope at him. It slapped against his chest and he caught it. "Get it?" I yelled. "Nothing is yours, Frank, but you act like everything is yours."

He drew and released a breath through lips pursed as if to kiss. I waited for him to speak and grew angrier and angrier when he didn't.

"Say something, Big Chief Writing Tablet." I wadded the Nebraska letter and threw it at him. "One, you're not a Native American; two, unless you've found the mother of all loopholes, there's no way you'll have a degree by August; and three, since when did you care about Native American studies?"

"It's your fault."

If he'd punched my nose I would've been less flabbergasted. "You stole my essay and lied to the fucking University of Nebraska: How the fuck is it my fault?"

He bellowed, "How's a roofer going to buy Nikes?" and then made a noise between sobbing and retching.

"What are you talking about, *Nikes?*"

"*I don't want to be a loser.* I took that essay and applied for that fellowship because I want our daughter to have Nikes—or whatever—and I want to be a professor, not a construction worker, and I want to be a good husband like my dad was for my mom and a good father like he was for me and Harmon."

My righteous indignation left me like a fart. I picked up the letter from Nebraska and smoothed it out on the table, then went to Frank and hugged him over the globe of my belly.

"It's okay. We'll figure it out."

No one had seen my essay with his name on it. There was no way he could pass himself off as Native American, no way he'd have a Ph.D. by August, and therefore no way he could accept the fellowship. The trouble was abstract but his contrition appeared real.

"We'll figure it out."

Frank pulled away and wiped his nose on his sleeve. "They almost kicked me out."

"I know."

He looked surprised. "Does everybody?"

I shrugged. "I just started talking to Joanie again, and all she and I talk about is the baby."

"We hardly ever talk about the baby."

"I didn't want to stress you out."

"I'm a complete asshole."

My emotions were spinning so quickly—pity to guilt to anger to pity—that I felt nauseated. "Zöe says you write poems about me. Is that true?"

"I'm going to read this." He picked up my battered yard sale copy of *What to Expect When You're Expecting* from the kitchen table. "And this." From beside the bed he fetched *What to Expect the First Year.* "I swear to God I'm going to read every page."

"Good, you should—but I want a poem."

Frank tucked the guides under his arm and woke up the Mac. He pushed in a floppy disk and after a few mouse clicks, the printer hemmed and hawed. He handed the poem to me and walked outside.

Lamplight, hair aflame, in dark Tennessee
Moths and tiny flies, glittering flecks of silver,

Haloed your brow.
The soft noise of powdered wings sounded in your ears.
Cicadas ratcheted in the trees.
Ithaca's air lacks Nashville's liquid waver:
Objects hold their quiet shape.
The moths and flies have been transported
To the night sky where they shine in patterns
Invisible to all but schoolchildren
Who see geometry wherever they look.
No longer haloed by bugs, stars follow you.
You hide your burning hair, but it's no use:
The stars love you too much.

Out the window over the kitchen sink I saw Frank shivering on the top step of the porch stairs, reading dutifully the guide to pregnancy and childbirth. He flipped a page and studied a line drawing of a fetus in its mother's womb and I wondered if he was scamming me when he claimed he'd stolen my essay because he wanted to be a good father and husband. I hoped not. I hoped when he said he did what he did so Ava could have Nikes it was because I'd forced him to admit something important, that he'd offered a deep truth about why he was who he was. I hoped the poem was a secret he'd shared with me, not a trick—surely he hadn't written untruthful poems about how he much loved me because he knew someone would tell me about them? He thumbed through the thick book to the index and I realized I might never know. Perhaps I was foolish to trust him, but I wanted to trust him, and so I decided to trust him. I wanted to believe his woes were simple—dead mother, dead father, dead brother—so I could soothe him.

34

With six weeks to go, I was bored with pregnancy. I no longer marveled at not tipping over, or at never feeling less than ravenous no matter what or how much I ate, or at yearning to have sex while simultaneously fearing while we did it I'd see Frank make a face betraying disgust with my hugeness.

The semester, like my pregnancy, moved glacially. I wrote my papers weeks before they were due in an unsuccessful attempt to fight off the monotony of the days. Except for attending class, I was done by April Fools'. With nothing else to do, I snooped. Frank's essays (I learned by double-clicking) were neither as bad nor as good as I'd feared. He'd done A-minus work for which he received A-minuses. There were no poems saved on the hard drive and I couldn't find the disk off which he'd retrieved the one he'd given me. I watched the films he made for his silence independent study and marveled at the sight of the sleeping skinny girl I'd once been. On the days he took the camera with him I checked to make sure the cassette labeled *SILENCE* was still in the shoebox filled with cords and other tapes.

In the middle of April—a month to go—I asked Frank why he was taking the camera almost every day and he confessed he was working on another film project. When he wouldn't tell me what it was about, I pouted.

"It's a surprise," he said, and then appeared to realize how dangerous that might sound. "A *good* surprise. I'm not in trouble, I promise."

"I didn't think you were," I was happy to tell him. My trust in him hadn't wavered since the day I'd found my stolen essay in the mailbox and confronted him. How could he not mean it when he said he wanted to be a good husband and father like his dead dad had been?

Frank read every pregnancy book I had, then bought more. I worried soon he'd be lecturing me and concocting new systems, but he didn't. He made a couple of checklists—what to pack for the trip to the hospital, what to have in the pantry when the baby came home—but the books told him to make those lists, and he didn't exhibit the kinds of mania I'd seen in the past: scrubbing a skillet until its nonstick coating flaked off, bending and re-bending all the forks until they stacked perfectly. I had to suggest we tour the maternity ward, buy Onesies, walk the diapers-and-baby-food aisles of Wegman's. Pointing to a box of rice cereal, he told me, "I like that kid's fat face." If he'd been worried about these things I would've worried, but he wasn't worried. He acted as if there was nothing odd about birthing beds, tiny shirts, and vegetables reduced to pastes. At Lamaze class he cracked wise and flirted while the other dads looked ready to puke from fear. His calm calmed me.

Nightly we did it in front of the TV on which we could see ourselves doing it. After, when we lay palely illuminated by the television's portrait of us in bed, Frank snoring lightly and twitching in his sleep, the baby kicked and kicked and kicked.

35

I packed boxes to kill time and then had to unpack when I needed a pencil sharpener or a stapler. One morning I opened a carton looking for toenail clippers, and before I could fold the flaps back down, Frank was standing over me. "You put paperbacks and steak knives together?" His lecture would've insulted a toddler: *books go with books, knives with knives.* When he went to campus the next day, I emptied all dozen boxes I'd filled and made in the middle of the room a hodgepodge of novels and wooden spoons and CDs and saucers and cups and screwdrivers and long underwear and knitting needles and basketball cards and old Dr Pepper bottles and skeins of yarn and spools of Scotch tape and curling ribbon, then divided the jumble into a dozen smaller piles and put each into a box I sealed with many lengths of packing tape.

I was ready to flip the calendar from April to May, give birth to Ava, move upstairs. Ithaca's mild and bright spring surprised me though I knew it was coming—hard to believe in the sun's return after months of sky the color of dirty slush. In the morning I took my mug of coffee to the little triangle of park at the end of Farm Street so I could watch a nanny named Ellie exercise twin toddlers named Sadie and Maddie. I basked in the sun and watched the little girls harass their endlessly patient pug Otto. "You should thank Jesus you're not having two," Ellie told me one breezy day. As if cued to explain why Jesus deserved my thanks, Sadie and Maddie each took hold of one of Otto's back legs and pulled in opposite directions. He squealed and Ellie snatched him up and held him under her arm. The girls listened to Ellie's explanation of how Otto was a baby and they needed to be gentle, then they began chasing each other while mimicking the dog's cry of agony.

When I got home, Frank was almost done assembling a crib. "Surprise," he said.

I was impressed. I'd been gone for an hour at most. "Where'd that come from?"

He held up a sheet of instructions. "IKEA. I had Todd buy it when he went home last weekend."

I kept to myself it might've been wise to wait until we'd moved upstairs before putting the thing together. "It looks great," I told him instead.

Frank twisted a screw with a tiny hex wrench and shook the crib to test the tightness. "You don't wish I'd gone into the woods and cut down a tree, milled the boards by hand, and built a bassinet?"

"Save your energy. I hear tell living with a newborn will be tiring as milling boards all day long." I ran my hand along the crib railing, then patted my belly. "I can see the shape of a foot when she shifts, but this is kind of freaking me out more than that."

He put his arm around me. "My hands started shaking when I opened the box."

We stood staring at our baby's bed.

36

My doctor reminded me of Wes Owen all grown up, which was at turns calming, worrisome, and funny. Archie Mock had Wes's sandy brown hair and scrubbed good looks and he wore the same wire-rimmed glasses Wes had worn when he was in high school. Like Wes he cut his eyes to the right to avoid peeking at my nudity. Like Wes he nodded when I talked. Like Wes he expected me to laugh at his dumb jokes. Waiting on the crackling paper sheet for Dr. Archie, I sometimes closed my eyes and thought of Wes and how scared we'd been I'd get pregnant if we weren't careful. The first few times we did it he pulled out even though he was wearing a condom. Later we were a little less uptight, but we'd always check expiration dates stamped on the rubbers' wrappers. It was hard for me to believe high school was only six years in my past.

I had a morning appointment the day Frank was to screen his new film, another project for Kierkegaard. My right shoulder started to ache the night before, and I was rubbing it when Archie came into the examining room.

"That hurt?"

"I must have slept on it wrong. Or picked something up wrong."

"Any lower back pain?"

I snorted. "Since, what, January? Maybe December?"

He nodded and marked my chart. "Let me get some blood and urine." Dr. Archie grinned Wes's grin. "Blood and Urine. I was into them before they went mainstream. I have their first EP on purple vinyl."

I dutifully snickered.

I went directly to campus after the appointment and was surprised to find the lecture hall nearly filled. Kierkegaard waved me over and moved his briefcase from the seat he'd saved. Professor Jenks and Rick Whitfield were two rows down, signing forms. Frank was at the front of the hall fiddling with a VCR under the watchful eye of an undergrad who'd surely been president of his high school's AV club.

"You must be pleased," Kierkegaard said as I tried to get comfortable in the narrow seat.

"I'll be glad when it's over," I told him, assuming he was talking about my pregnancy. When he looked puzzled, I worried the movie we were about to watch included footage of me asleep, naked, and hugely pregnant.

Joanie and Todd came in and had to sit in the aisle—every seat was taken. I counted across a row and then up the tiers and estimated there were over a hundred people in the room.

"Is this another silence film?" I asked Kierkegaard.

"Oh. Well. Yes. *No*, I suppose is the answer to that question. Yes, *No* is the answer."

The lights were dimmed before I could ask another. Frank stood at the podium and adjusted a microphone, then nodded to the AV kid, who pushed *play* on the VCR. A PixelVision image of the downtown post office was projected onto a screen behind Frank. Enlarged to that size, the grainy picture looked like it had been recorded with a surveillance camera. The surveilled citizens of Ithaca walked up and down the P.O. steps, dropped letters into the mailbox, fed coins into parking meters, checked their watches.

Frank's amplified voice filled the lecture hall. "A few months ago my cousin told my wife my great-great grandmother was Native American."

On screen Frank walked into the shot wearing a feather headdress. I was relieved to see I wasn't the nude, unconscious star.

"Her name … was … *Susan*."

His pseudo-profound tone triggered scattered laughter, then shushing.

In front of the post office, Frank tried to hand out leaflets, but no one would take one.

"My father never mentioned Susan was Native American."

An older woman walking a dog offered Frank spare change and he accepted it.

"It's not clear what tribe Susan belonged to. My cousin says our grandfather told her Seneca most often, but sometimes claimed she was Flathead."

Two hippie kids carrying guitars stopped and talked to Frank, accepted and read his leaflet, and shook his hand before sauntering off.

"Those are photocopies of treaties the U.S. Government signed with the Seneca and the Flathead—all broken.

"At first I treated the news of Susan like it was no big deal—most Americans must be at least a sixteenth of everything."

On the screen a policeman made Frank move three feet to the right.

"Then, I'm embarrassed to admit, I wondered if I could exploit Susan, scam something because my great-great grandmother may or may not have been Seneca or Flathead or Navajo or Blackfoot or Illini—all tribes my grandfather claimed Susan belonged to."

The cop eyeballed the post office's front door like he was triangulating and waved Frank over three more feet.

"But when I tried to find out what tribe Susan was really from, I couldn't. Maybe there's nothing sinister about that—I don't know what part of France or Wales my ancestors came from, and I don't figure that's because their children wanted to deny their parents were French or Welsh—but it feels sinister no one even knows what tribe Susan was from, doesn't it?"

A trio of frat boys wearing shirts emblazoned with Greek letters and carrying lacrosse sticks mocked Frank until he said something to them and then one of them slapped Frank's headdress off with his stick.

"A sixteenth is pretty diluted, I'll admit it, but after at first not caring, then caring for the wrong reasons, then realizing what a jerk I was for not caring and then caring for the wrong reasons, I started to wonder why I was still wondering what it means to be Native American."

Frank put his headdress back on and the same guy knocked it off again. One of his friends snatched a few leaflets and crushed them into a ball they began to toss with their lacrosse sticks back and forth over Frank's head. He pretended not to notice.

"Lacrosse is Native American in origin," Frank said.

A young woman pushing a stroller stopped to harangue the frat boys. One gave her the finger and the gang wandered off, still flipping wadded-up treaties to one another.

"I wonder why some tribes feel a sixteenth is more than enough to make me Native American, but others claim I'm a generation or two or three too far down the bloodline. I wonder what it means that my daughter will be a thirty-second, her children a sixty-fourth, theirs a one-hundred-twenty-eighth."

The woman with the stroller asked Frank a question and appeared upset by his answer. She mimicked his headdress with her fingers and shook her head as if disgusted.

"If it's true we all have at least a sixteenth of everything in us, does that make us all the same, or does it mean that we're all so jumbled there's no way any two of us can have anything truly in common?"

It started to rain on screen. People under umbrellas hurried past Frank. He kept trying to distribute his treaties, but they grew limp in his hands. The camera followed him as he walked down the street plastering them like broadsides onto the fenders of cars.

The screen went black and we all sat in darkness. The film was not lovely like his silence movies, which was disappointing, and his comments were simplistic, melodramatic, and heavy-handed. Nevertheless, I was moved. His allusion to my essay and his fellowship application sounded to my ear like an apology, albeit one in code, and hearing he thought about Ava beyond her birth pleased me at the same time it made me feel shortsighted. It was no masterpiece, I decided, but thank God he'd managed to fill a room and get some respectful attention after the debacle of being nearly expelled. When the lights came up, Frank was nervously sipping from a bottle of water. I smiled and gave him a thumbs-up. He looked away.

Rick Whitfield stood and turned to face the crowd. "Please join me in congratulating Frank Doyle. His is the first interdisciplinary dissertation project that combines work in creative writing, film and video, and American Indian studies."

A jolt of pain shot through my shoulder and I twisted in my seat. *Interdisciplinary dissertation?*

"Frank's impressive work has already earned him a post-doctoral fellowship at the University of Nebraska, a fellowship he'll take up as soon as his daughter is born—any day now!—and he and his wife, Hannah, move to Lincoln."

Rick Whitfield pointed and everyone in the lecture hall looked my way, Frank included. My mouth was hanging open and I shut it so quickly my teeth clicked. I forced a smile.

"Thanks, Frank," Rick Whitfield said, "for letting us see some of *Broken Treaties*."

When the applause began, my hands rose reflexively from my belly and came together for a single clap. I sat holding my own hand while people filed past to congratulate me on Frank's success, to wish me luck in Lincoln, to pat my belly. My right shoulder felt as if it was being crushed in a hot vice and I had to fight the urge to curl toward the pain. Admirers encircled Frank on stage.

"Help me up," I told Kierkegaard. I offered him my left hand.

"You're leaving?" he said as he pulled me to my feet. "There is to be lunch at Moosewood?"

"I need to pee," I lied.

I staggered to the Honda and drove off campus angry and hurting. The burning in my shoulder spread to my lower back and my stomach churned. He was a liar, a scam artist. *Dumbfuck,* I thought when I remembered the short moment in the dark I'd though he was apologizing to me and thinking about the baby, not himself. "Stupid," I said aloud when I saw in my memory Rick Whitfield praising Frank's lame movie. Then I felt stupid. They were getting rid of him. They didn't really think his movie was enough to earn him a Ph.D., but it was worth being able to claim his success as theirs and to rid themselves of an annoyance.

I was confused, then. Who was to blame? Frank for finding loopholes? Whitfield and Jenks and Kierkegaard for signing forms? When I turned off the car on Farm Street, I looked up at the stop sign down the block and couldn't remember once braking on the way home, or the colors of any of the stoplights.

The apartment was filled with the boxes I'd packed thinking we were moving upstairs. The answering machine blinked its code for two messages and I pushed the button. The first was from my mother, wondering in a worried voice where I was on a Wednesday at noon and hoping all was well. The second was from Dr. Archie.

"Hannah, I ran some tests. Um, why don't you come have that baby *right now*. I'm not kidding. There's a lot of protein in your urine, and that aching shoulder and lower back might mean your liver's in trouble—did we talk about preeclampsia? You need to get to the hospital, ASAP. My nurse'll let them know you're coming."

I called my mother and said, "I'm having the baby today," as soon as she answered.

"What? You're not due for weeks. What's happening? Let me talk to Frank."

"Fuck you, Mom!" I hollered. "*Fuck* you and *fuck* Frank." I hung up and ignored the ringing that began almost immediately.

I found Moosewood's number in the book, lifted and slammed down and lifted the receiver until I heard a dial tone and not my mother's voice, and dialed. The hostess curtly told me the Whitfield party had not arrived.

"I need to leave a message."

"No can do, sorry."

"Sure, right, thanks, listen, when they get there, tell the Injun with Professor Rick his wife went to the hospital to have the baby, okay? His name's Frank—my husband the Injun, not the baby." I hung up.

He'd packed my overnight bag and prepared me a non-perishable snack in a paper sack on which he'd written my name. What more did I need from him?

I wished I were in labor, that halfway to the hospital I'd have to pull over and a grizzled cop or a hippie midwife would stop and catch Ava. Instead I listened to the Pixies and thought I could feel my liver pulsing in time with "Here Comes Your Man." I parked and walked through the lot, pausing to lean for a moment against a doctor's yellow Mercedes convertible when it felt like someone was easing an icepick between my shoulders. A sullen orderly too short for his beard and pushing a wheelchair wide enough for two moms met me at the reception desk and rolled me to the maternity ward.

My nurse was young and olive-skinned and in her pale green scrubs looked like a model for nursing school brochures. She helped me up from the giant's wheelchair and into a bed from which I could see the shimmering lake.

Waiting for the epidural to take effect, I thought about how for nine months my worries regarding pregnancy, childbirth, and motherhood had been constant but unspecific, sometimes so unspecific I worried I was too dumb to worry correctly. The books all comforted: everything was normal. Often I wished for a checklist of ten or twenty or a hundred important things I could worry about. Instead my worries were a dull and unending ache, much like the one at the base of my spine that kept me awake at night. Watching the sunlight sparkle off the surface of the lake like shining from shook foil, I admitted to myself why I'd been unable to choose ten or twenty or a hundred things about pregnancy, childbirth, and motherhood to fret over: each of those ten or twenty or hundred worries was twisted around a worry about Frank. I closed my eyes and untwisted a few worries about the baby from a few about Frank and when I separated them, each sparked like a live wire.

He arrived panting as if he'd run from Moosewood. There was celebratory gin on his breath.

"Who held the camera for *Broken Treaties?*" was all I wanted to know.

"Todd. Are you in labor?"

"Nope, I've got preeclampsia."

"What does that mean?"

I shrugged and looked out the window. Two canoes full of kids were following the near shoreline. "Means you didn't read the pregnancy books you said you did, I guess, or you'd know what it means."

"Is the baby okay?"

I nodded, still watching the lake.

"Are you okay?"

I nodded again, refusing to look at him.

"What the fuck is wrong with you?"

I sighed. "My husband's a liar and a cheat, I'm moving to Nebraska, I'm suffering from a serious medical condition, I'm about to have a baby via emergency Caesarean. What's wrong with me? Pick one, Frank. Hey, dude, why not pick two?" With the bedside remote I turned on the TV and wondered how drugged I was. It appeared to be receiving a live feed of the kids in canoes I could see out the window.

Ava's birth was nightmarish in concept—horizontal scalpel slash, organs shoved aside to allow for a vertical slash, baby plucked out like the parasite she technically was—but, thankfully, less horrific in execution. Drugs helped. I was given the choice of mirror or no mirror and chose no. Ava's removal felt like being shaken by a moment of turbulence—then there she was, slimy and mad, bigger than I'd imagined her, though when Dr. Archie put her in my arms she was impossibly small. Ava snorted and threw a tiny punch and I felt my ribcage gently turn inside out to allow my ballooning heart to inflate with joy. "Jesus," I said reflexively. I put my thumb on Ava's chest and felt her miniature heartbeat.

Archie had to cajole me into letting go of my baby so he could stitch up my wounds. "Dad can go with her to the nursery," he cooed. Later, in recovery, Demerol drip dimming my pain, I was able to recognize how overwhelmed I was by the love I felt for Ava now that she was off in the nursery breathing and crying and pursing her tiny mouth. It felt as if hours and hours had passed since I'd watched Frank follow the nurse carrying Ava out of the delivery room, but the clock swore this was not true. I was about to buzz for help when he slowly wheeled in the clear plastic bassinet. Ava wore a green cap with a tag on top that looked like an apple's stem.

"I gave her her first bath." His voice was full of amazement and adoration.

The nurse lifted Ava and set her in the crook of my arm. Frank gasped, then said, "Look at her eyelashes."

I touched her tiny mouth and Ava sucked my fingertip.

"Look!" Frank told the nurse. "Look at that!"

I sent Frank home the first night and refused to speak to him the next morning. The nurse acted as if this was normal and I delighted in Frank's discomfort. Joanie and Nat and Sam came after lunch with flowers and I thanked them by saying, "You're more thoughtful than Frank. He hasn't gotten anything for me or for the baby. Could you tell him I'd like a glass of water?" After a tense twenty minutes of praising Ava's cuteness and passing messages from me to Frank, they excused themselves.

"Are you going to leave me?" he asked when they were gone.

I hadn't considered this option, but it sounded too good to dismiss without some thought. "Maybe." Ava mewled like a kitten and I snuggled her closer.

"Listen, I know I fucked up when I took your essay, but the good news is I also fucked up and didn't put on enough stamps, so basically nothing happened, and I know you think *Broken Treaties* is bogus, but you have to understand, I'm not as smart as you are."

"That's your apology? You didn't affix proper postage and you're not as smart as I am?"

He sighed and rubbed his eyes. "What's to be gained by mocking me?"

"I don't think anyone's going to gain anything today," I said, unsure exactly what that meant. Ava began to fuss and I had to swallow hard to stop myself from crying.

Frank walked slowly across the room and sat down in a chair in front of the window. "Are you going to leave me?" he tried again.

I took deep calming breaths through my nose while I pondered the question. If I'd believed Frank was the only one to blame the answer would've been easy, but loopholes are also snares. If he'd claimed to be Catholic to get Ava into a good kindergarten, would I think him a terrible man? Probably not, so why was I so disturbed by his false claims of Nativeness made to get a two-year fellowship? Sadly, it wasn't hard to believe my diligence and ethics were abnormal in academia, and if that were true, how could I blame him for being normal? Even his argument about the stamps had some validity. His crimes lacked victims. And then there was the simple fact I loved him enough to marry him and have his child and he loved me enough to marry me and want me to have his child.

"I need time to decide." It was a lie; already I was imagining life in Lincoln. "Go away and come back tomorrow morning."

37

My mother arrived in Ithaca the day we came home from the hospital, four days after Ava was born. Frank and I were exhausted and alarmed we'd been trusted to leave with the baby. "Don't these people know who we are?" he asked me in the parking lot, only half joking. We'd just spent ten minutes instructing each other how to loosen and tighten the straps of the car seat while Ava looked wide-eyed at the lake, the sky, the squirrels in the trees—or was blinded by morning sunlight and not yet smart enough to squint. When we got home we couldn't get formula to come out of the bottles Frank had carefully sanitized but not tested. Ava wailed as we shook them and squeezed the nipples and considered going to the ER for help. We barely heard my mother knock. Frank opened the door and held out a bottle when he saw it was she. Mom twisted off the top, removed a disk of plastic—"Prevents leaks when traveling," she explained—twisted the top back on, and handed me the bottle. Ava's crying stopped when I plugged her mouth with the now-functioning nipple.

"Thanks, Dot," Frank said, but my mother didn't hear him. She stared at the baby in my arms and moved her lips like she was sucking the bottle.

"You want to feed her?" I asked.

While she held Ava and grinned like a fool, I cheered, "Frank won a fellowship and we're moving to Lincoln, Nebraska!"

She didn't look away from her granddaughter, didn't stop smiling, but she sounded heartbroken when she asked, "Why didn't you tell me before?"

"Unexpected sudden good fortune. Frank only heard last week, and then the baby came."

Frank thanked me with his eyes.

"I know Nebraska's a long way from Nashville," I told her, "but so's Ithaca. And it's only for two years. After that we might be a lot closer. Who knows?"

She nodded but wasn't really listening. Ava had mesmerized her.

My mother's motel room was twice the size of our apartment and wasn't filled with moving boxes. After I spent Mom's first day in town lying on her king-sized bed petting and kissing Ava's bald flat spot while Frank ran errands, my mother suggested he and I stay there and she sleep on the Farm Street futon.

"I'm sorry I said *fuck you*."

She smiled and shook her head. "I already forgot that."

Living in the Super 8 with Ava was like rehearsing a new life. The next four days, while my mother was in town and paying for the room, Frank and I slept with the baby between us on the huge, soft mattress. We changed her diapers and bathed her in the sink, smelled her head, and watched her breathe and poked each other and pointed when she pursed her lips or stuck out her tongue or kicked in her sleep or coughed. I quickly forgot how I'd managed to fill the minutes and hours before Ava was in my arms, or in Frank's, or asleep in the middle of the big bed inside a fort of pillows. My mother came three times a day with food, stayed a few hours to hold the baby while we ate, answered our questions, agreed Ava was perfect, then left us alone.

Each day moving to Nebraska seemed more and more like a good idea—a place to start anew now that Ava had made us new. The morning my mother left town Frank rented a U-Haul and paid two Cornell wrestlers he'd tutored to fill it with our boxes and furniture. We spent one last night at the Super 8 eating Indian carryout and watching Ava stare at wilting balloons Mom had bought her five days earlier. A draft I couldn't feel made them quiver, and her tiny eyes widened and followed their movement.

38

We headed west at sunrise. Frank let me pick the route and I took our little family on a tour of ruined Midwestern industrial cities: Erie, Cleveland (he blew it a kiss and sped up), Toledo. On the second day we followed I-80 along Indiana's dreary northern border and the edge of Chicago's southward stain—poor careworn Joliet. Ava slept so deeply I poked her awake every hour to make sure she hadn't slipped into a coma. The U-Haul's cramped cab worried me. The cramped apartment led to systems, and I feared strategies for aiming AC vents, tuning the radio, caring for Ava, and angling mirrors to reflect proof we still towed the Honda. Instead Frank was laidback and sloppy, Coke cans and Fritos bags on the floor, no method to his choice of FM. When we lost a station, he spun the loose dial like a wheel of fortune and listened to whatever came from the buzzing speakers: classic rock, political rant, single-A baseball, bluegrass, NPR.

In La Salle we stopped at an Exxon so I could change a rancid diaper. Frank and I laughed about the stink. We were in it together: parenthood, moving, Lincoln. He filled the U-Haul's echoing tank while I fed Ava a bottle of formula and looked at the atlas and the long blue sky over the cornfield edging the gas station's parking lot, a sky and cornfield I imagined stretched the 450 miles between where we were and where we were going.

39

Frank rented a duplex sight unseen and from the curb it looked like he'd made a serious mistake—tiny twin 1960s ranches conjoined by a two-car garage, ours the right ranch, a *For Rent* sign in front of the left—but when I opened the unlocked front door I found fresh paint, new curtains, and a *WELCOME HOME!* Hallmark card on the spotless kitchen counter. Our new home smelled of carpet shampoo and Pine-Sol. Beside the greeting card was a paper plate loaded with oatmeal cookies and sealed in plastic wrap. The bathroom gleamed, even the grout around the tub, and a Mason jar of homemade potpourri sat atop the toilet. The smaller of the two bedrooms was painted pale pink and in its windows hung white curtains on which purple butterflies flew. Ava was fussing and had been since she woke us before dawn in the La Salle motel.

"Look at your room," I cooed, and she began to cry as if I'd slapped her.

"Mr. Doyle told me baby girl," a man said behind me. I was so startled I almost dropped Ava. I turned to a smiling retiree. "Dan Hampshire," he told me when I shifted my wailing baby girl to my left shoulder and shook his hand. "Wife told me pink," he called over the noise. "Got to be pink."

"You're the landlord?" I was discombobulated by travel, the spotless rooms, Ava's keening.

He nodded. "Live down the street. Saw your husband carrying boxes and thought he might need some help. Got a son and some grandsons coming over."

"Pink's perfect."

He grinned at Ava even though she was screaming. "My four—all boys. Not even a granddaughter."

Frank and three generations of Hampshire men unloaded the crib first—in which fussy Ava magically went to sleep when I lay her down—then quickly emptied the truck and sat on the bumper of the U-Haul drinking pony Budweisers. Frank looked like a cousin, but I heard them call him "Professor Doyle." It was not yet noon when they left. We ate oatmeal cookies for lunch and I drank the last little beer, my first in nine months, and then took a quick hot shower with the door cracked so I could hear if Ava woke. She didn't, so I had time to find a clean shirt and brush my hair. Frank already had the Mac up and running on the desk in the bedroom. It would've been a better idea to put it in another room, but I feared he'd explain a system if I suggested he move it, and the past days had been blissfully free of systems.

When I came out into the living room I found him opening one of the scrambled boxes I'd sealed in New York. He saw me standing in the doorway and held up my paperback *Lolita*. In his other hand he held a potato masher. I braced for a lesson on packing.

"You were reading this the day I met you."

I was touched he remembered. He didn't say anything about the potato masher and I was doubly touched. Someone banged on the screen door and Ava resumed crying.

I went to soothe her and when I brought her back to the living room Frank was smiling uncomfortably at a balding guy in plaid sport shirt. "Hannah, this is David!" he nearly yelled.

"B-u-g-g-e," the guy spelled. "David Bugge." He grimaced at Ava, nodded at the hand I offered, and turned back to Frank.

"So, tell me the theoretical framework of your project?" It sounded like a test question, not chitchat. Bugge was shaped as if he were wearing a down vest under his madras short-sleeve: head too small for his humped shoulders, arms too puny for his voluptuous chest and generous middle.

Frank laughed nervously. "You read my application, right?"

"Assimilation?"

"Assimilation! Exactly! Man, I can't believe I'm this tired from the trip. The baby woke me up at four."

"And then you drank all that beer with the Hampshires from down the block," I muttered from the kitchen. Bugge ignored me and Frank gave me a pleading look. I filled a bottle and gave it to Ava. I was mad at him for being weak at the same time I felt sorry for him for feeling he needed to dissemble.

"I warn you," Bugge told Frank, "Lincoln is no Ithaca. The first day I arrived from Palo Alto I wanted to slit my wrists—everyone does when they first get here—but you learn to live with the corn and the beef and the football. And the locals can be charming."

I filled my voice with fake wifely cheer and said, "I'm from Nashville and Frank's from Cleveland."

Bugge looked puzzled. "But you were at Cornell, right?" he asked Frank.

"We both were," I said.

Bugge squinted at me through his thick glasses like he couldn't figure out who I was. Ava farted and he shuddered. "You were an undergrad?"

"I'm finishing a dissertation on women's Indian captivity narratives and theatrical enactments of Indian captivity." I figured Frank knew better than to contradict me.

"That sounds a lot like what Frank's doing. Is he your mentor?"

I left Bugge to torture Frank and sneer at Nebraska, slammed the bedroom door behind me. In the mirror I saw

I wore a chevron of Ava's snot on my chest. The bed was heaped with baby shower loot, and from the pile I retrieved the Over-the-Shoulder Baby Holder, a brightly-pattered sling Nat and Sam had given me, looped it over my shoulder, and gently dropped Ava in. When I gave her the bottle, she put the nipple in her mouth, closed one wise eye, and narrowed the other and sighted down the barrel of the bottle like she was aiming her gun. I looked for a box I'd marked with three stars and found it in the corner, still taped shut.

I heard Bugge leave. Frank opened the bedroom door and nonchalantly said, "Sorry about that," like we'd been interrupted by a Jehovah's Witness ringing the doorbell. "What were we talking about? Nabokov?"

"Have you opened a box with big envelopes?" When he left the room, I ripped the tape from the box in which I'd packed the essay he'd tried to steal. I slid it into the sling beside Ava.

Frank came back with an envelope in each hand. "They were packed with my Nerf football, a brick, a handful of dead double-A batteries, and a stack of junk mail."

I glared at him, daring him to say something else, and when he wisely didn't, I said, "Pen?"

He felt his pockets and passed me a ballpoint.

"I'm going for a walk to the post office."

"Sorry about Bugge," he tried, but I didn't answer.

Dan Hampshire was riding his lawnmower when I walked up High Street. He cut the engine and tipped a yellow mesh cap on which an ear of corn with wings took flight.

"Can you point me toward the post office?"

He scratched his chin. "Give you a ride?"

I imagined puttering there on the John Deere. "It's a pretty day, and I've been in that U-Haul for a long time. I could use the walk." I adjusted the sling so he could see Ava. "We could use the walk."

He gave one short nod. "High to north on South 48th to east on Van Dorn and the P.O. is right after South 51st. There's a park on either side of Van Dorn right there. You could sit and rest."

I hadn't been lying when I said it was a pretty day. The sun was out but it was cool and breezy. Without Ava's warmth against my chest and the exertion of lugging her eight pounds, I would've been shivering in my T-shirt and shorts. Eleven nondescript blocks later I walked into the low brick building and addressed the envelope to the journal Frank had tried and failed to send my stolen article—the address was burned into my memory, even the zip code. No cover letter; instead, I wrote *Hannah Guttentag* on the top of every page and my new address on the back of the last. I wanted to mark my turf more than I wanted the editors to publish the essay.

I waited in line behind an old man who called the postal workers by name. There was a high-pitched din everyone was laughing about, a sound I felt I should be able to recognize. "Afternoon, Red," one of the guys behind the counter called to me, grinning sweetly. He looked like Dan Hampshire's meaty brother.

"What is that *noise?*" I asked.

"Chicks." His nametag read Pete. "Gross of baby chickens."

"You can send chicks in the mail?"

"Yes, ma'am. Chicks, earthworms, lizards, snails, crickets, grasshoppers. I forget anything, Stanley?"

"Bees," the next postal worked added. "Queens have to be shipped overnight. Just like adult roosters and hens."

Pete and Stanley weren't kidding.

"Got a baby in there?" Pete asked.

I slid the envelope across and adjusted the edge of the sling so he could see Ava.

"Little girl?"

I nodded, distracted by what the envelope held. "Proof of delivery?"

"No problem." He pointed at my chest. "You go to Cornell?"

"I'm working on my Ph.D.," I said, ready to be insulted by a man who special-delivered worms and honeybees.

"While raising the world's cutest baby? That's crazy!" He laughed kindheartedly and I was weirdly thrilled. He handed me a receipt and told me to bring Ava back soon. On my way out a curvy young blonde with hair down to her waist who I did not know pointed at my Cornell shirt and waved like she recognized me. "Hannah? Hannah Doyle?"

I wanted to correct her—Hannah *Guttentag*—but didn't. "Yes?"

She beamed. "I'm Lizzie Huckabee. I'm at UN-L."

My heart sank. "I need to change a diaper," I fibbed, and fled before she too could treat me like I was Frank's underling and erase the happiness I'd felt when Postman Pete was nice to me.

At home the books were shelved, the plates were in the cupboards, the bed was made, a load of laundry was in the washer, and all the boxes had been broken down and stacked in the garage beside the Honda, biggest on the bottom of the stack, smallest on top. My C-section stitches burned. It'd been a bad idea to walk so far. Frank wasn't in the house and hadn't left a note. I checked the bedroom closet and saw in the neat row of sneakers a gap where his running shoes would fit.

40

It was impossible for me to stay angry with Frank or Bugge because sleep deprivation made it impossible to hold any thought, let alone a grudge, for more than five minutes. Ava was colicky. The pediatrician Dan Hampshire's wife recommended showed up at my door to tell me this, and though he made a house call and was kind to me and called Ava *little angel* while she shrieked in his face and did not ask me to pay him a dime, I wanted to punch Dr. Olsen's big red nose when he told me no one really knew what colic was and there was no pill or injection or suppository that would cure her and make her sleep. "Nap when she naps," he prescribed, then showed me The Colic Hold, told me sometimes running the vacuum helped, and suggested I take her for walks. I had to count in my head to keep from slamming the door behind the nice old M.D. when he left. I held my baby upside-down, limbs dangling; I ran the Hoover; I put her in her stroller and pushed her around the block. She cried.

I found some surprising solace in Frank's systems. Rows of bottles stood ready in the fridge, sanitized and filled with formula while I napped on the rare occasions Ava napped. The clothes I dropped wherever I struggled out of them disappeared and reappeared clean and folded in the drawers of the Goodwill dresser I found below the window one afternoon when I woke alone in the beige bedroom. Frank was on campus from nine to five. He called each noon to tell me he was on his way to eat lunch with another adult and I hated him for the five minutes I could focus on being jealous. When he called at quitting time to tell me he was on the way home, for five minutes I hated him for not being home already.

When we left Ithaca, I told myself I'd see how I felt about academia after a year in Lincoln, a year taking care of Ava and deciding what was truly important to me, but after two lonely weeks, I sent Pat Caldwheel a letter begging her to help me figure out how I could remain enrolled even though I was a thousand miles away from Cornell. I told her I'd realized how much the degree meant to me. I kept to myself one reason it meant so much was that I'd told David Bugge and Pete the Postman I was working toward it, and unlike my husband, I didn't lie. She sent back forms for me to sign, reading lists, a timeline, and for Ava a stuffed elephant and a tiny *Ithaca is GORGES* T-shirt. I looked at her plan for me—deadlines, requirements, assignments—and saw that when Frank's fellowship expired, I would have a Ph.D., and it would be my turn.

41

On the third Saturday in June there was an English department picnic. We'd been in Nebraska for three weeks and
boredom and isolation made me willing to suffer hot dogs
and Cokes with Bugge. As we drove, I realized I hadn't paid
much attention to Lincoln on the day we came to town,
the only other time I'd been farther than the grocery store.
There was something calming about its uniform lack of flash.
It was like so many towns that grew steadily after World
War II—brick ranch houses, brick schools, brick libraries,
neighborhood parks with swings and hobby horses on giant
springs—but with lots of railroad crossings, and grain silos
on the horizon and sometimes even right next to a school
or a playground.

When we pulled into the park, Frank admitted he knew
there was going to be a croquet tournament pitting graduate
students against untenured professors. "I figured you wouldn't
come if I told you."

I looked at the group looking at us sitting in the car and
recognized Lizzie Huckabee, the woman who'd introduced
herself at the post office. I knew how much this meant to
Frank, so I shrugged and smiled. "Could be fun," I said, and
he squeezed my knee gratefully.

I lifted Ava from the car seat and strapped her into her
stroller and followed Frank across the grass. The cooler in the
picnic shelter was full of cans of Diet Sprite.

"No beer?" I asked a skinny woman in plaid Bermuda
shorts. "No way I'm playing croquet sober."

Bugge looked up from sorting wickets and mallets and
said, "A, the lack of alcoholic beverages is in accordance with
the regulations for public parks in the City of Lincoln, and

B, since you're neither student nor faculty at this university, technically you're not welcome to play."

I waited for him to raise an eyebrow, grin, wink, give me some sign he was joking. Instead he made himself reach out and pet Ava's downy head with two trembling fingers. "And C, you shouldn't be drinking anyway, should you?" He ogled my boobs to make clear his point.

I smiled and stuck them out. "Well, B-u-g-g-e Bugge, A, I don't breastfeed, so I'll drink what I want, B, before you ask, it's none of your business why I don't breastfeed, C, only a complete loser would want to play croquet sober, and D, only a tool would quote the bylaws of the City of Lincoln, Nebraska Department of Parks and Recreation."

Someone tapped my shoulder before Bugge could counter with another lettered list. "Can I hold the baby?" Lizzie Huckabee asked. She wore an ankle-length denim skirt though it was over ninety degrees, and I wondered if her outfit and her long hair had religious significance.

Thunder boomed in the near distance. "Sounds like rain," Frank said, and everyone nodded solemnly at his Native American wisdom.

Faculty was ahead five wickets and Bugge was braying from the rulebook when the clouds finally opened and ruined the tournament. Ava was in Lizzie's arms, untroubled by the storm. In fifteen minutes I'd learned Lizzie was a Lincoln native and had been east of the Mississippi only once—a senior trip to Chicago where she visited the Shedd Aquarium and the Museum of Science and Industry and saw from a bus window the Picasso in Daley Plaza—and never west of Denver, where she went every Thanksgiving to visit her father and stepmother, had graduated from Nebraska Wesleyan though she was not a Methodist, not anything, really, though she thought she believed in a higher power, was studying Great Plains literature at UN-L, and writing a dissertation on Native Americans in Willa Cather novels. I was breathless just listening to her, grateful she filled the silence since anger and fatigue tied my tongue.

Lizzie looked down at Ava smacking her tiny mouth while dreaming of a bottle. "It must be wonderful to be a mother."

"It is," I confessed, happy she appeared to envy a part of my life that didn't feel very enviable. "I feel stupid when I try to explain, though. It's like sex, you know? The only ways to talk about how great sex is are either corny or stupid or clinical."

She nodded. "I'm a virgin." She wasn't defensive or ashamed. It was just another fact, like her star sign—Aquarius, she'd told me.

"That's cool." I wondered if I was the only person in academia who'd had sex before grad school, let alone before graduating from high school. It would explain why everyone I knew in Ithaca was so horny.

As if she was reading my mind, Lizzie asked, "What's Cornell like?" Her tone was dreamy and awestruck and I had to sip Diet Sprite to keep from giggling.

Frank was loudly pretending to hate organized sports on the other side of the shelter and we turned to listen. "Just look at the mascots. Seminoles? Redskins? Braves? Give me a fucking break."

Lizzie put her lips to my ear and confessed, "I know I shouldn't, but I love college football."

Her breath was hot and guilty and it nearly made me swoon. I lifted sleeping Ava from her arms, walked to Frank and passed him the baby, then went back to Lizzie and took her hand and dragged her into the rain, across the sodden croquet ground, and to the cover of an empty picnic shelter. A half-deflated Cookie Monster balloon swung over the detritus of a kid's *Sesame Street*-themed birthday party.

"I'm sick of listening to that bullshit," I told her. "He's a Cleveland *Indians* fan."

"Hannah," Frank yelled through the downpour. "The baby's awake and wants a bottle."

"So give her a bottle," I yelled back. "Your squaw needs a break."

I realized I was still holding Lizzie's hand and let it go. I knew it was pathetic, but I wanted someone to think I was cool, and so I told her anecdotes about Cornell parties while Frank fed Ava and glared at me. The wine tasting at which two female grad students got into a fight about whether the pinot noir evoked the memory of white or yellow flowers and the one arguing for yellow had her heart broken when the married professor who was sleeping with her sided with the one who claimed the flowers were white; the party to which everyone had to wear bridesmaids' dresses; the Halloween party before which Frank spent days crafting his crow-head and at which he smashed the mask when he got drunk and fell into Rick Whitfield's sunken living room. I turned skinny-dipping with Todd and Joanie and Nat and Sam into a party. Weed, Miller High Life, nudity in the woods—close enough.

"But after a while they become the same party," I claimed as the storm slowed and I could hear Ava fussing. "Smart people read too much, think too much, drink too much, and everybody ends up with a headache."

Lizzie laughed, but she looked impressed.

Ava's napping was an excuse for angry silence in the car. At home Frank whispered, "Take a break," and carried the baby into her room. It was supposed to be an apology, I understood, but it backfired. The break allowed me to realize how seldom Frank cared for Ava. No wonder I was so tired. In the middle of the night I paced the floor with her because he needed to be able to get up at eight to go to campus. Every retired or jobless man in the neighborhood owned a leaf blower, and from nine to three they took turns blowing who knew what—the ashes of my burned thoughts?—while Ava made noises that sounded more like devious snickering than the pained complaints of a colic sufferer. Frank called at noon to taunt me with the news he was on his way to lunch without a baby, called again at five to remind me he'd been away all day, then came home and sat on the couch with Ava. They watched the local news, Frank drinking a PBR, Ava a bottle, while I made dinner. SpaghettiOs, hot dogs and tater tots, Kraft Macaroni & Cheese: our palates had grown dull as toddlers'. We sat behind TV trays and ate barbeque-flavored chips and sleeves of store-brand chocolate chip cookies with and after every meal. Then Frank passed me Ava, closed the bedroom door and read for an hour. He went for a long run, took a shower when he got back, and washed the dishes. It was after nine o'clock before he offered to hold the baby again.

I heard Ava fussing and ducked into the bathroom, locked the door, and turned on the taps—my first bath since the C-section. While the tub filled I flossed my teeth and shuddered when I realized it was the first time I'd flossed in Nebraska. I soaked in water so hot it would've injured Ava, shaved my stubbly legs, my shadowed armpits. I slid down until only my nose broke the surface and I heard Ava's crying wobble through the water, then dim, then stop. My fingers and toes were wrinkled when I arose from the tepid bath ten or twenty or thirty minutes later. Losing track of time was a novelty and I savored it. I cut my nails, plucked my eyebrows, flossed again.

I wrapped my head in a towel and put on a pair of Frank's sweatpants and the T-shirt he'd laid out for his evening run. When I peeked into Ava's room, I found him sitting on the floor beside her crib, legs folded into half-lotus, hands resting on his knees, palms up, fingers forming okay signs. His eyes were closed and he was in the middle of reciting *Goodnight Moon* from memory: "Goodnight little house. And goodnight mouse . . ." Ava was snoring. I backed out of the doorway and went into the bedroom.

The sheets were clean and smelled of fabric softener and exhaustion pressed me into them like a lover.

I didn't hear Frank get into bed, but I woke when he whispered, "Everyone's like Bugge. All day long I have to act like Tonto. They'd love to see me cry over a garbage dump or put my ear to a railroad track and tell them the train's coming. It's all bullshit, but I'm going to tough it out, and it'll pay off when I get a good job."

I felt bad for him and so I didn't tell him about the thick envelope from Pat Caldweel and my two-year plan.

"I'll help more with the baby," he swore.

42

Lizzie started coming over almost every weekday morning around ten. She'd grown up with five little brothers and changed Ava's diapers without pausing from conversation. For an hour or two we would sit and talk about nothing important—Nashville, Lincoln, sci-fi books we read as teenagers, horns we'd abandoned in college (Lizzie had been first-chair trombone in high school, I'd played pep band cornet)—then she'd drive me to lunch in her hand-me-down grandma Buick in which, for Ava, she'd installed the hand-me-down car seat a nephew had just outgrown.

We were not students at the same school. Lizzie tickled Ava and gave her a bath in the kitchen sink but didn't seem jealous I had a baby and she didn't. It was an easy and un-complicated friendship, just the kind I needed since I was so tired and lonely. Her timing couldn't have been better. After a few calm hours spent in her company I was able to remain sane when Frank came home full of systems.

One night he decreed the allowable number of sheets of toilet paper was four for pee and eight for shit. The next morning he freaked out when he found a hole a mouse chewed in a box of instant mashed potatoes. Frank called Dan Hampshire and demanded he bring traps, which Dan did, apologizing to me as he set them, gob of peanut butter on each. A few hours later Frank phoned from campus to find out if the mouse had been killed, and when I suggested mice were nocturnal, he said, "I'll check on that." Lizzie and I laughed together when I hung up the phone and told her he was going to do some mouse research. When he got home, he searched the baseboards for droppings with a Xeroxed page of illustrations he'd made to help him identify mouse poop.

For two weeks he kept his promise to help more, and he was preparing a bottle for Ava when he called me into the kitchen and pointed into the sink at the plate on which the crust from my breakfast toast rested.

"Think like a mouse. You have to think like a mouse."

"And goodnight mouse." I was sure he'd get the joke.

He stared at me. "What?"

"Never mind."

I took the bottle and carried Ava to the couch, closed my eyes and listened to Frank wash the plate, sweep the floors, and tie the garbage bag. Since he'd promised to help more he'd stopped hiding in the bedroom to read every evening. I reminded myself how disappointed he was, how exhausted Ava made us both, how much I loved him. The baby fell asleep and I took her into her room and lay her in her crib. I watched her breathe, marveling.

Frank was in the kitchen, jerking opening cupboards as if he thought he'd catch the mouse by surprise even though he'd been banging flatware and dishes for twenty minutes.

"Shut up," I told him when he opened his mouth to tell me again to think like a mouse. I got down on my knees and unzipped his fly and he put his hands in my hair and leaned back against the sink and spoke not a word.

43

Things settled down. The mouse didn't trip a trap and get its neck broken, but it didn't chew any more boxes or drop any more little turds along the baseboards, and Frank stopped demanding I think like anything other than his wife. The blowjobs helped, surely. Lizzie took me to campus to get a visiting scholar's library card. In the blank for *Sponsor*, I wrote B U G G E, spacing the letters as a joke.

The undergrad behind the desk raised her eyebrows when I slid the form to her. "That guy's a total dick," she said, then put her hand over her mouth and pointed at Ava in the sling. "Sorry for the swear."

I checked out a reprint of the second edition of *The Goodness and Soveraignty of God* and a dozen books from the list Pat Caldweel sent, and while Lizzie bathed Ava and enlightened her about each piggy's role, I read the first pages of Sarah Weed's narrative and felt the little machine at the back of my brain sputter, backfire, and begin to hum. *I was many Removes into the Wilderness, and all was gone—except my life—, and I knew not but the next moment that too might be gone as well—but still I was Hopeful & Faithful.* When I read the printer's version of the raid—brave Samuel shooting one Indian and clubbing another before being shot in the back by "a cowardly Salvage"—I remembered every single word of Sarah's description of her husband frantically searching a chest of his mother's clothes for a disguise.

44

On the morning of the Fourth of July I jerked awake sure Ava had been kidnapped. Dawn lit the bedroom window and she wasn't crying. When I went into her room, she was holding her feet and staring at the ceiling so intently I looked up to see what was there: light fixture. Worried she was suffering some severe version of colic that left her too weak to fuss, I called Dr. Olsen and told him she'd slept through the night. "Should I take her to the ER?"

His laugh sounded old-fashioned, too jolly for the end of the century.

For a week it'd been 100 at high noon and one day it reached 106. Frank had to run before eight. I met him at the door when he came back. He was panting and soaked in sweat. The AC had already kicked on, though it wasn't yet seven thirty, and he shuddered when he stepped over the threshold. "It could come back," I told him, "but it looks like the colic's gone." Frank hugged me.

We hid from the heat with our freakishly calm baby and waited for dusk. Frank watched three or four overlapping baseball games while I read the Bowdlerized version of Sarah Weed's travails. I knew the first edition well enough to recognize where it'd been changed, but my memory didn't need to be that good, so clumsy were the printer's swapping out of Goody Weed's idiosyncratic complaints for generic sanctimony.

There was a party on a farm outside of town where Lizzie's dissertation director lived with her husband, a watercolorist who painted cows. Lizzie begged me to come, swore Bugge wouldn't be there—"Too rustic for him"—and promised pie.

How could I refuse pie? Ava didn't cry once all day and didn't make a peep when I belted her into her seat. We drove out Nebraska Highway to a little town called Cheney—grain elevator with a faded Purina checkerboard sign, tractor repair shop, schoolhouse, three paved streets with little houses under old trees.

At a mailbox with a balloon tied to it we turned off the pavement and onto a gravel road that led over a set of tracks and into a tallgrass meadow. A quarter mile ahead a grove of trees rose from the swatch of prairie. We passed a falling-down outbuilding filled with shadows of wheelbarrows and lawnmowers and a garden filled with tomato plants overtopping their cages. In the middle of the trees was a clearing in which cars were parked haphazardly on the mown lawn of an old foursquare farmhouse painted mint green with lavender trim. I'd expected a brick rancher.

Everyone was in the kitchen drinking beer and eating watermelon slices. Frank was by far the youngest man there, and Lizzie looked like she'd been dragged to a party by her parents, but everybody was laughing and having a good time. From the other room I heard the clunk of a record falling from the changer onto a turntable and the hiss of the needle catching the first groove. Lizzie introduced me to Harold, the painter, and to her dissertation director, Fanny.

"Watch that melon," Fanny told me, raising her voice to be heard over Jefferson Airplane. "It's soaked in rum."

I cringed in anticipation of a lecture on booze and breast-feeding.

"Tastes like shit," she said instead.

"Rotgut," Harold lamented. "Try the pie—no busthead in it."

It was raspberry and delicious.

Grace Slick yodeled about truth and lies and when all the joy inside you dies.

"I *picked* those berries!" Fanny hollered over her.

I peeked at Ava in the sling and knew I was looking into a mirror—her eyes were open wide at the noise. I hadn't been around so many voices in months. Frank appeared not to know anyone in the kitchen, but Lizzie was leading him from group to group. Another piece of pie and a beer later I started to feel overwhelmed and wandered out of the house and toward the quiet garden. A dog followed me, a huge old greyhound I'd noticed lurking outside the screen door. Under a buzzing security light I stopped to scratch her ears and she stuck her nose into the sling and sniffed Ava. At the edge of my vision there was a flash of green. I turned to it and saw a blue starburst, then a red flower—fireworks off on the horizon. I walked toward them, stepping from the circle of light into darkness. The white dog was luminous and I followed her when she passed me and trotted toward the distant show. She led me to a fence separating mown grass from waist-high corn. I watched tiny explosions over Lincoln and heard the noise of firecrackers coming from the direction of Cheney.

The section of Sarah Weed's narrative I'd read before we left for the party described an evening she strayed too far from her captors' camp while searching for groundnuts and got lost in the dark woods. Even though she'd been sent to find food, she feared the Indians would assume she'd tried to escape, and when she found her way back or was found by them she'd be punished, perhaps killed. She detailed her worries—beatings, scalping, loss of faith, devils and monsters in the dark, never again seeing her sister or her daughters, safe in Provincetown because they were visiting their aunt when the raid occurred. Just as the fear of never getting out of the woods eclipsed her fear of being murdered by her captors, she saw the flicker of their campfire through the trees and thanked God for Light in the Darkness.

The dog grumbled and I looked over my shoulder to see Lizzie unsteadily heading in my direction. "What're you doing?" she asked, her breath rank with discount rum.

"Fireworks." I pointed. "Here comes the grand finale."

We watched Roman candles explode miles away. A bottle rocket screamed nearby.

"It's a shame being pregnant and having a baby steals your sex drive," she said, and I wondered for a moment what the connection to the fireworks was, then understood she was drunk and there was none, she was just thinking about sex.

"As if. I was horny the entire time I was pregnant. Soon as I sobered up from the epidural, I was horny again."

She looked shocked and I laughed at her prudery in spite of myself.

I watched a final purple comet illuminate the smudge of smoke on the horizon and didn't tell her that while Ava napped in her crib an hour before we left for the party, Frank kissed my neck, reminded me how many weeks had passed since the C-section, and showed me how to lie on my side so he could get behind me and not push against the incision—sometimes his library research was helpful. It was quick and clumsy, but thinking about it made me want to go home and do it again.

45

The next morning, when Frank went for his run, nostalgia made me hunt for the PixelVision camera and the silence tape. Our return to sex had been a relief, but I felt fat and old, and the heat exhausted me if I even stepped outside, and I wanted to see myself thin and young and asleep in winter sunshine, and I didn't care if wanting to watch myself when I'd been thin was narcissistic. The camera was on a shelf in the bedroom. I found the shoebox of cords and tapes in the closet. Ava was in the living room in a hand-me-down baby swing Lizzie had brought over, and she watched me plug in the camera through half-shut eyes. *Broken Treaties* was on top of a rubber-banded stack of four cassettes, the other three all labeled *Silence/Copy.*

I closed the curtains and put a tape into the camera, turned the little black-and-white to channel 3, and pushed play, expecting a streetlamp illuminating snowflakes. Instead I saw myself, hugely pregnant, on all fours, Frank behind me. He'd lied when he told me the camera wasn't recording. My face was loose with bliss and my breasts and my big, hanging belly shook each time he bumped against my jiggly butt. I was embarrassed I was clearly having a good time and embarrassed when I remembered how I'd enjoyed watching myself have such a good time. I punched stop when I remembered Ava was aimed at the television. The swing had put her to sleep, thankfully.

I ejected the tape and put in another with the same label, hoping this time I'd get silence but fearing another record of one of the many nights in Ithaca Frank and I screwed in front of the TV which showed us screwing. When I started the next tape, the picture was turned as if the camera had been on its side when it was recording. I tipped my head and looked at a tidy black-and-white bedroom with a framed poster of Van Gough's "Starry Night" hanging above a brass bed with Laura Ashley sheets and dust ruffle. For a moment I thought I was looking at a silence film I didn't know about, one perhaps commenting upon the bliss of domestic silence, one that showed how happy Frank was as a father and husband—and then he led Lizzie into the room.

He was in his running clothes and she wore men's plaid pajamas. She looked slimmer when not wearing a big T-shirt and a long skirt, her usual uniform. They sat on the bed and talked, then he put his hand on her leg. My neck was getting stiff from watching sideways, so I got up and tipped the little TV onto its side, righting the picture. Ava was still asleep in the swing.

Frank was talking and Lizzie was frowning and nodding while he slid his hand slowly up her leg. She stopped nodding but kept frowning when he unbuttoned her PJs. Her boobs were bigger than mine, her nipples darker and larger. She frowned when he pulled his shirt over his head, frowned when he kicked off his shoes, frowned when he stood and pulled down his shorts. She looked away from his crotch, looked back, looked away, frowning. He sat beside her, naked but for his socks, erection pointing to the ceiling, and there was more mute earnest talk. Lizzie kept nodding and frowning, slumped forward as if embarrassed to be shirtless.

He stood and bent to pick up his shorts and for a second I was sure the discussion had led to an agreement this was a bad idea, but then he took a condom from his pocket. Lizzie wiggled out of her plaid pants without getting up, then scooted backward onto the bed and lay down on top of the sheets, frowning. Frank climbed in with her and eased her knees apart and she said something and I read his lips when he nodded and said "Okay." Her frown tightened when he tried to push in, tightened more when he lifted himself slightly and looked down and used his hand to force himself into her. The pain on Lizzie's face was disturbing. Not only had Frank cheated on me with my friend, it was pretty clear he'd filmed her deflowering. On the little TV Lizzie's skin was the color of a corpse's, and her tightly closed eyes and her complete stillness made her look even deader.

Ava burped and when I looked up, she was awake and watching Frank and Lizzie fornicating. I covered her eyes and lifted her from the seat and rushed her into her room and lay her on the floor and flipped through bright board books that made her eyes open wide, spun a rainbow-colored pinwheel an inch in front of her face, made ten finger puppets dance so close to her that she blinked rapidly. I wanted to erase from her limited memory the sight of her father fucking Lizzie Huckabee.

Had his claims of innocence been lies, part of a seduction system? It'd been nice to skip the braggadocio and shame brought on by comparing lists of former lovers, but had Frank duped me with a clichéd sex fantasy I now feared I shared with innumerable women and men: hot virgin, quick study in the bedroom, nobody's lover but mine, mine, mine?

I heard what sounded like an air raid siren when the front door opened, and when I walked out into the living room, Frank was watching the tape of himself on top of Lizzie. He turned it off when he saw me.

"Did she know about the camera?"

"No."

The sirens rose and fell. "What the hell, *Frank?*"

"I think a tornado's coming."

"I don't mean that, Frank, I mean *what the hell*—Lizzie?"

"She has no idea who I am." He said it like this was a legitimate defense for adultery.

"Neither do I, Frank."

"Why are you saying my name over and over?"

I was unsure exactly why I was, but pleased it bothered him. "I don't know, *Frank*. Why do you think I am, *Frank?*"

He shrugged his fucking shrug and I picked up the camera and swung it as hard as I could and hit him in the face. It broke at the handle and the tape flew across the room and went skittering along the kitchen linoleum. Blood came from between the fingers he pressed to his cheek.

"Get the fuck out of here!" I yelled.

"It's raining!" he yelled back.

Ava started to howl in the other room, matching the siren's pitch. I showed him the jagged edge of the camera's handle and promised, "I'll cut your fucking pig throat, *Frank*."

I locked and bolted the door behind him and went to Ava and hugged her while she cried harder than I could ever remember her crying before. I held her to my chest and I could feel her screaming buzzing inside my bones. I hated Frank for having sex with Lizzie, but I hated him more for taping it, and I hated him most for exploiting my exhaustion. There was no one on campus to impress by being in his office all day long—it was summertime. I'd been too tired to remember that for weeks he'd supposedly been working hard to impress the people I watched Bugge introduce him to for the first time at the picnic. At the farm in Cheney he knew no one, and at least half of crowd were English professors. If I'd been sleeping, I would've been suspicious since May, but sleep deprivation made me trust him. My trust gave him the opportunity to do what he'd done with Lizzie, and to do it who-knew-how-many times. I'd been stupid to hope fatherhood and a new zip code might make a new man of Frank.

Thunder shook the house violently and long enough for me to fear a tornado was bearing down, and as I ran with Ava to the windowless bathroom, lightning cracked so loudly I thought the roof was being torn off, then there was a moment of frightening silence, and then hail pounded down on the shingles and hammered the gutters and drowned out Ava's laments. She calmed as the storm calmed, and thirty minutes later I opened the front door to a landscape covered in pearls and ping-pong balls.

Down the street the blue lights on a sheriff's car flashed brightly, calling attention to the darkness at noon. Bob Hampshire was talking to a deputy and pointing in my direction. The cop drove the hundred yards between our houses. He turned off the lights when he got out.

"Mrs. Doyle?"

My mind wasn't working right. I was sure Frank had committed a crime, and I considered claiming I didn't know any Mrs. Doyle, but I was innocent and I didn't see Frank in the back of the car.

"Sure."

"I'm sorry to have to ask you this, ma'am, but is this your husband's shoe?" He held up a Nike with a red swoosh.

"Size eleven?" I asked, still wondering if I was going to be charged as an accessory to God knew what—Lizzie's rape? The deputy checked the tongue. "Yes ma'am, eleven."

"Okay," I agreed. "It's his."

He was maybe twenty-five, but under his Smokey the Bear hat he could've passed for fifteen. "Ma'am." He paused and looked over at Bob Hampshire pretending to sweep hailstones down his driveway while spying on us. "Ma'am, it appears like your husband was sitting at a picnic table under a tree, and it appears like the tree got hit by lightning, and, ma'am, he's dead. Your husband is deceased."

"Picnic, lightning? Seriously?"

The deputy nodded. "Yes ma'am, it appears."

"Like in *Lolita?*"

"Ma'am, I'm sorry but I'm not sure what that means, 'Like in Lolita.'"

"So Frank just told you to say that and he didn't explain?"

The deputy looked like he was holding back tears. "Ma'am, your husband was deceased when I got—when help arrived, and because of that, he didn't tell me—he didn't tell anyone to say anything to you. There were no last words said."

He reached to take my baby away from me and I tried to jerk her back but my arms didn't bend the way I expected them to and my knees buckled and for a moment I was looking up into the weird dim bruise-green sky. When I came to, Dan Hampshire and the deputy were kneeling beside me, the deputy fanning me with his silly hat. Betty Hampshire was holding Ava and my tiny daughter looked at me with worry in her infant's eyes. It wasn't a joke about Nabokov's novel or a reference to the day Frank met me in Ithaca when I was reading that book or to the day he unpacked the paperback in Lincoln when it felt like everything was going to be okay, finally. Frank had been struck by lighting and he was dead.

Betty Hampshire led me into her living room and sat me down on a scratchy brown couch and fetched me a can of Fresca and held my hand. I was too stunned to think. Ava grunted and I looked down at her in my arms and it took me a beat to remember she was my child.

"I think she might need to be changed," Betty said.

I nodded—I could smell Betty was right—and stood up. She didn't let go of my hand. "I'll be okay." My voice sounded like a robot's.

"You should call someone," Betty suggested.

"My mother?"

She squeezed my hand until I pulled it from her moist grip. "I'll check on you," she promised.

Lizzie was in the kitchen of the duplex washing my coffee mug when I came in. "The door was wide open." Her smile faded as I stood silently staring, thinking of her pained face and Frank moving mechanically between her legs. "What?"

"Frank got hit by lightning and he's dead."

She squinted and cocked her head and I felt worse for her than I did for Frank. "I don't get it."

"He got hit by lightning and he's dead."

When Lizzie began cry, I went to her and hugged her, Ava pressed between us. I waited to feel sadness well up in me, waited to hear my sobbing join Lizzie's, but instead I felt weirdly relieved. I didn't have to forgive Frank this time. I could hold this grudge forever. I decided not to tell Lizzie about the tape as she sputtered and shook against my shoulder. "It's okay," I lied. "It's okay."

46

The morning after Frank died, I called Pat Caldweel and left the news on her answering machine, and she called back two hours later to tell me she'd gotten me a teaching assistantship for the fall semester. She'd also found me a place to live. A friend of hers who taught in the philosophy department had an apartment over her garage. "Two bedrooms, full kitchen, a tub in the bathroom—it's a big garage. And she's willing to reduce the rent if you feed her cats when she goes out of town."

It was a better offer than the one my mother proposed the night before: *Come home to Nashville and sleep in your old room and maybe be a substitute junior high English teacher.* I called Mom back after Pat Caldweel said to me, "It'll be so good to see you and baby Ava," and told her I was going back to Cornell. "They know me there," I explained. "I like it there." What I didn't tell her was I was still mad at Frank—or why I was mad—and in Ithaca at least they knew Frank had been a cheat and a liar, even if they didn't know about Lizzie.

I called Lizzie next and told her I needed some time alone. Even while she was crying and then trying to soothe me on the day Frank died, all I could think of was the sight of the two of them in bed.

"Call me if you need to talk," she said. "Or if you need me to come over and help with Ava. Or if you need *anything.*"

"Sure," I agreed.

Alone with the baby, I watched Ava more closely than I ever. Her tiny fingernails and her fat knees dumbfounded me. I felt like a bad mother for not paying enough attention before. The day after Frank died I put her down only to change her diaper and that night I slept on the floor beside her crib. The next day I had graham crackers and Diet Coke for breakfast so I wouldn't have to put Ava in the car seat to go to the grocery store, or ask someone to bring me something and then suffer even a moment of polite divided attention when they arrived. Betty left a casserole on my doorstep but ran away after knocking. When Lizzie called and asked if I needed anything, I told her no, thank you.

That afternoon a teenager dressed like a janitor delivered a box of Frank's ashes. His driver's license identified him as an organ donor, news to me, and the hospital waived the cremation fee when I gave them permission to take whatever they could. The lightning burned his left ear going in and scorched off the hair on his left ankle going out. His heart and his eyes were destroyed, but everything else would save lives, I was promised. I put the box in the garage. That night I was sure I heard my dead husband's voice in the dishwasher's gurgle and bump.

Early the next morning I packed. I ignored the careful stack of broken-down boxes Frank had made and filled the hatchback with layers: my books on the bottom, my pots and pans and spoons and forks and knives next, then my clothes, laundered and folded or hung on hangers by Frank, and Ava's baby gear on top. My Mac rode shotgun. I almost forgot the box of Frank's ashes on the dryer. It fit neatly in the glove compartment.

I abandoned his clothes, including the shoe the deputy asked me to identify, the crib he'd assembled, the futon on which we'd slept and wrestled. I left Bob Hampshire a check written on the account into which the university had deposited Frank's first stipend the day he was killed. On the memo line I wrote *Sorry*. I called Lizzie and told her I still didn't feel like company, but I'd see her the next day, maybe, and then I unplugged the phone and put it in the car. I drove east along the same roads that'd taken me west two months before, and Ava and I were back in New York on July 10, 1992.

47

It took less than a day for me to understand I'd been foolish to believe in Ithaca Frank's death and my new widowhood would be overshadowed by a shared vision of him as a cheater and fake, a vision, it turned out, no one would admit sharing with me now that he was dead, not even Pat Caldweel, who referred to him as "Poor Frank." His debts had been forgiven when lightning struck. Now I was the only one who thought he was a dick. I considered telling Professor Caldweel about Lizzie, but then I'd have to tell her about the fight and about how I'd chased Frank out the door while the sirens wailed, and I worried she'd think I was lying about Lizzie, that I'd invented a dramatic reason for sending Frank to his death because I felt guilty for throwing him out after a fight about something stupid. I couldn't tell anyone.

Joanie had left town to take a job in Ohio, Nat and Sam had broken up, and Todd was living with the woman who'd argued the flowers she smelled in her wine glass were white. When I ran into my friends, they looked weird, like people who resembled people I once knew, and they stared at Ava in her stroller like they'd never seen a baby before. Every time I was on campus I was sure people were whispering behind my back. I went to a playground hoping to meet other women with kids I might befriend and for my troubles received a tongue-lashing regarding my choice of disposable diapers from a fat hippie who drove a Range Rover and had to pause from her attack on me to stop her twin four-year-old boys from pissing off the top of the jungle gym. After that I spent my time with my landlady's cats. She'd gone to Montreal for ten days to visit her octogenarian mother, and I had free roam of the house. There was no TV, but she had an amazing collection of 1970s and '80s pop albums, so Ava and I passed our days listening to Queen and Rush and Duran Duran and Eurythmics and petting Roland Barthes and Jean-Paul Sartre, the two Siamese.

One afternoon, a week or so after I'd returned to Ithaca, I was at the co-op grocery, standing before a shelf of organic cat food trying to match the flavors on the list my landlady had left with the flavors on the cans, when behind me a boy's voice said, "Hannah?"

I turned to find Kree Carey, dressed only in flip-flops and a green bathing suit he'd pulled down low on his hips to expose a wide white belt between trunks and tanned belly. He'd grown nearly a foot taller, and his hair was long and blond and pretty. Mark came down the aisle and pulled up his son's pants like a bully giving a wedgie. "Jesus, Kree, what's your plan? Expose yourself to the dog food?" He looked up at me and said, "Hannah?" just like Kree had.

I smiled and nodded to them. "Hello, Carey men."

"Whose baby?" Kree asked, peeking into the sling at Ava.

"Mine."

Mark looked taken aback.

"How's Helena?"

Kree hooked his thumbs in his trunks and pulled them down farther than they had been before.

"Well," Mark said, "here's the thing, we're no longer husband and wife, but we are committed parenting partners, so that's good. She, you see, she, well, she ..." Mark cut his eyes at Kree while the kid pretended to read the ingredients on a bag of kitten food. "She found the charms of another too much to resist." It was a euphemism so clumsy it was lovely, one that seven-year-old Kree might not know the meaning of, but I guessed he had a pretty good idea based on the context—*no longer husband and wife, but committed parenting partners.*

"Where's your—" Mark started to ask, then appeared to recognize how the question might sound if I didn't subscribe to heteronormative contracts even as liberal as committed parenting partners.

"He found the charms of another too much to resist."

Mark's smile was sad, and when he invited me out to dinner the next night, I accepted without thinking.

48

After insisting I let her watch Ava when I went out, Pat Caldweel hired a sitter to help. "I know you trust me, and I think I'd be able to handle it, but what if I can't figure out the diapers or the pacifier or something?"

I laughed and said goodbye to Ava and my friend the professor and her grinning teen helper and walked out the door without my baby for first time since she was born. I sat in the car for eleven minutes watching the digital clock's numbers change. I worried about Ava and then to stop worrying about her I worried about what I was wearing: a short-sleeved white cotton blouse with a Peter Pan collar, a purple silk skirt that stopped above my knees, white low-top Chucks without socks. Fretting about whether my shoes were too casual allowed me to manage to turn the key and drive away. Mark met me at a little café and we sat in a booth and drank a bottle of cold white wine and ate eggplant and buffalo mozzarella sandwiches and talked about wine and water buffalo cheese and eggplants and varieties of olive oil and did not discuss adultery.

We were two glasses into a bottle of peppery red when he reached across the table, petted my cheek, and said, "Motherhood has been kind to you."

"Fatherhood's done you right," I told him, and rubbed my ankle against his. I was drunk and happy. He moved to my side of the booth and put his hand under my skirt and ran the tip of one finger up and down the inside of my thigh while I tried not to pant or giggle into my wine.

We kissed on the sidewalk and I decided my two options were make out in the car or go home to Ava—though I'd have to walk, as much as I'd had to drink.

"I want to make love to you," Mark gasped in my ear.

I thought about my scarred belly, about how the last peek of sex I'd had was seeing Frank and Lizzie. "I can't. I'm a mess."

"No you're not," he said firmly. "You're a real woman."

"Let's fool around in your car," I suggested.

He led me to his ancient VW Squareback and when I unzipped his fly, he started the engine. "Please," he moaned. "I have to have you in bed."

I reached into his pants and squeezed. "Beg me again." He was too intent on the road to speak. He raced along, my hand still in his pants, and when he ran a red light, I worried we'd be killed or pulled over and arrested and Pat Caldweel would have to identify my body or bail me out. We made it to his house alive, and when he set the brake, I gave him another squeeze and said again, "Beg me."

"Please," he groaned.

The bedroom was exactly as I remembered it—framed sketches of nudes from Mark's undergraduate art school days, the calico curtains I'd helped Helena hem the summer I lived with them—and because it hadn't changed I felt a jab of guilt, as if I'd traveled back to 1990 and I was about to sleep with the married man whose wife once paid me to care for their son.

"It's 1992," I said out loud.

"That's right," Mark concurred. "Now lie down."

I did, wondering why we weren't undressing. I worried I'd misunderstood what was going on and he expected me to sleep off the wine—then he lit a candle on the dresser and turned off the lamp. He pulled my underwear down over my sneakers and when he touched the inside of my thigh, I spread my knees. Mark got into bed, knelt before me, flipped up my skirt, and bent and kissed me between the legs. I moaned and closed my eyes. When I counted backward through July, I was shocked it'd been only thirteen days since Frank and I had sex, a dozen since he'd been killed. I opened my eyes and watched the candle's wavering light on the ceiling and tried to concentrate on how good what Mark was doing felt.

"You have no idea who I am."

He slipped two fingers into me and disagreed: "Hannah, Hannah Guttentag." Suddenly every muscle in my body was clenching and releasing those fingers as an orgasm shook me without forewarning.

"Get on top," I huffed.

He didn't wear a condom and I didn't care. Mark slid into and out of me and I unbuttoned his shirt buttons and he unbuttoned mine. I was happy my bunched-up skirt hid my slack belly, but I wished he would take off my bra. The bedsprings below me sang a song I remembered hearing from the next room and every nerve in my body sparked as I moved against him. He thrust in a careful way that made me sure he'd seen my scar and knew not to hurt me—but not so carefully I didn't feel another orgasm brewing. His hairy legs scratched my thighs and the bush between his legs felt fantastic when he rubbed it between mine. I wanted him to make me feel this good forever. When Mark braced himself on his elbow and fumbled with my bra, I understood he was as excited as I was, and that made me even more excited. The clasp popped and he bent his head and I heard a cough from the little room in which I used to sleep. Mark sucked my nipple and the jolt of pleasure made me grind against him even as I asked him, "Who's there?" fearing it was Kree.

"Helena," he said, changing nipples. I felt the same jolt, but this time I was able to stop my body from responding.

"She still lives here?" I tried to wiggle out from under him, but he pushed into me and pinned me to the bed with all his weight. The pain in my guts made me yelp. He pressed harder and I choked down a scream.

His eyes were closed while he bounced against me to made the bed squeak. "She always joked about how you could hear us fucking, and now the bitch has to listen to me fucking you." I tried to shove him off and he grabbed one of my nipples and twisted as if to tune me back to the horny frequency I'd been on before Helena coughed. He kept humping me until I grabbed his balls and clenched them as tightly as I could. He shrieked and rolled off me and I heard Helena crying or laughing or both as I snatched my shirt and staggered out of the bedroom clutching my throbbing stomach. I tripped over the edge of the living room rug and nearly fell across the coffee table where my purse sat. Out on the porch I found I held Mark's shirt, not mine, but I put it on and buttoned it up and tried to stop crying.

I stumbled drunk and wounded into a night I'd known before, one filled with fireflies and buzzing bugs. It was the same night I'd led Frank to the park, and as I walked through the unchanging evening, it seemed I'd been cursed to live forever in a single summer night in Ithaca. I supposed the pain that made me stoop and hug myself might slowly dim and perhaps vanish, but I was sure the pain of watching Frank atop Lizzie would fester forever.

It took me twenty minutes to baby-step the six downhill blocks to the Honda, each step hurting a little less than the one before. The car was half a block from DeWitt Park, and I retrieved the box of ashes from the glove compartment and set out to scatter them. First I dropped a handful of all that was left of Frank under the bench where once I'd jerked him off. When I sat down and closed my eyes, I saw the deputy holding up Frank's shoe. A low voice mumbled in the dark and I opened my eyes, expecting Frank's ghost. Instead a teenaged couple hurried past, hand in hand.

I was still too buzzed to drive, so I walked to the bungalow where Frank and I traded the stories of our lives. Behind closed blinds someone played an Al Green record and I had to sneak up and down creaking porch stairs to leave a pile of ashes. I hid behind a tree and looked at the swing and told myself there was no way I could've guessed what would happen after that night. I left a thin line of ashes along the kitchen windowsill of the little apartment we'd shared on Farm Street. There was no curtain, and when I peeked in I saw it was vacant, which made me sad and angry—I could've been living there, alone and happy.

Farm Street's murmuring TVs led to Linn Street's barking yard dogs which led to the head of the trail that bent along the creek and rose up the gorge. I trudged the slippery path for a few hundred yards until I reached the pool where I used to take Kree to swim. There, where he'd first spoken to me, I dumped the last of Frank. I stood in the dark beside Cascadilla Creek, naked under my skirt, braless under Mark Carey's shirt, worried he had ejaculated inside me. When I rubbed my nose and smelled soot, I realized I'd just inhaled some of my dead husband, a realization that made me weep into my gritty hands.

Alone in the woods, I remembered the thanks Sarah Weed gave God for her numerous afflictions. The censoring printer hadn't changed a word of her narrative's last pages, and like the conclusions of almost all stories of captivation and rescue, those pages were full of happiness and praise and hope I'd once judged delusional and simpleminded and pandering, but when I thought of Ava, strong and pink and perfect, I recognized Sarah Weed and the other captive women weren't crazy or stupid or playing to the crowd. Life was, is, and always will be hard, but even in the midst of darkest winter there are sunny days, days like the one Frank recorded in my favorite of his silence films—the day I lay asleep and untroubled and warm after he held me—each of those days a blessing compared to weeks and months of darkness and cold. Sarah Weed taught me to *praise the Cold and praise the Dark and praise Tribulations for they make sweeter the sunlit days of Happiness.* How could I be certain there weren't dozens and dozens of sweet, sunlit days to come? I dipped my hands into the cold water, washing away the last of Frank, and then I followed the creek back to civilization and back to my daughter.